Johnny Dead

Two years earlier, manhunter John Deletéreo had been ambushed by masked killers. He, his wife and unborn child perished under the hot New Mexico sun, with two simple graves on a hillside the only testament to their demise.

When a man by the name of John Deletéreo rides into Payton's Bluff seeking answers to a mystery plaguing him since birth, townsfolk think they've seen a ghost. Legend calls him Johnny Dead, a man with a skull-carved Peacemaker who delivers grim justice and then vanishes into the western night.

Now, events have been set in motion to kill a man many claim isn't even alive. . . .

Johnny Dead

Lance Howard

A Black Horse Western

ROBERT HALE · LONDON

© Howard Hopkins 2005
First published in Great Britain 2005

ISBN 0 7090 7757 2

Robert Hale Limited
Clerkenwell House
Clerkenwell Green
London EC1R 0HT

For Tannenbaum

Typeset by
Derek Doyle & Associates, Shaw Heath.
Printed and bound in Great Britain by
Antony Rowe Limited, Wiltshire.

CHAPTER ONE

You made a mistake . . .

The thought drummed through Kylie Barton's mind as she strode along the darkened trail leading from her small homestead to Payton's Bluff. She had made a terrible mistake and God would damn her for it if she weren't somehow able to reverse the events she'd set in motion.

Before a man died.

It didn't matter that man deserved whatever happened to him. Not a lick. It didn't matter that she despised him more than any other single human being – if he could rightly be called such – on God's green earth. It didn't matter that she'd let her hate seethe inside until it became a poison boiling in her soul. It only mattered that she had sent a telegram requesting the services of a killer, one who would likely scoff at any thoughts of reneging at this late date. He was riding from Texas, after all, on the promise of payment for a job rendered.

She touched the bulge the greenbacks made in her skirt pocket, shivered. Maybe he would accept payment and go about his way. Wasn't there a chance, even a slim one, that this could be stopped?

Another shiver rattled her. Fear crawled up from the pit of her belly and caused her to stumble in her step. A band of tightness clamped about her chest. The path wavered before her vision, as she grew momentarily light-headed.

Drawing a deep breath of the chilly autumn air to calm herself, she found it did nothing more than make her shudder uncontrollably. She wished she had dressed in something heavier than a blouse and skirt, but she knew that the chill would have penetrated to her bones even had she bundled up in layers of wool. Too much of the coldness swelled from within, frosted guilt at the steps she'd taken to right a wrong. Steps that warned her if she went through with what she'd planned she would be no better than the man she despised.

Wrapping her arms about herself she fought to rein her fear, but every tiny noise from the forest made her start.

An aspen leaf crackled beneath her high-laced boots. The hardpack held a varnish of frost and to either side the darkened shapes of ash and fir, maple and spruce, swayed under an iced breeze. Shadows distorted, weaving into menacing shapes that seemed to claw at her legs.

Edging just above the trees, the blood-colored October moon glazed the leaf- and pine needle-blanketed ground with tarnished light. Her breath puffed out in frosty ghosts.

Ky-lie . . .

She stopped, heart jumping into her throat, a small sound of fright escaping her full lips. Her amethyst eyes widened with worry, as she turned her head to peer at the trail behind her. A ribbony stretch of rust and black leading into the ebony distance met her gaze, but nothing else.

6

Head swiveling forward, she caught herself holding her breath and forced it out. Had she heard something? A whisper? She could have sworn it had come from somewhere behind her, a harsh hiss of a thing that spoke her name.

No, that was impossible. She was alone out here, alone and more frightened than she could ever recall having been before.

Except for that night . . .

She would have heard someone riding up, wouldn't she? The man who was supposed to meet her would surely have a horse; at least, she reckoned he wouldn't come on foot.

A crashing of brush made her start; she swore her feet came inches off the hardpack. Her heart pounded and she spun as the sound continued, retreating into the woods.

An animal of some sort. That was all it was. Nothing more. Only her shattered nerves inflated it into something threatening.

'You're scaring yourself silly, woman,' she said under her breath, hoping to convince herself she was jumping at shadows. The words provided her with little confidence or comfort.

Turning, she looked back in the direction of her homestead, but saw only darkened trail, a trail suddenly grown as sinister as the road to Hell.

'Why did you ever send that telegram, you stupid woman? Why did you go and make things worse? You could have just done what the rest did, let it go, let him get away with—'

Another sound stopped her murmuring cold. Another movement in the brush. This time she felt certain no animal made that noise. She froze where she stood, unable to force her legs to take another step, unable to draw a breath. Her mind began to reel and she feared she would collapse into a heap on the hardback, quivering like a child in terror of the dark.

You're stronger than that, Kylie Barton. You have to be. You can't let it happen again. Never again. . . .

Her gaze swept across the edge of the forest. She forced herself to breathe and the sour stench of decaying leaves clogged her nostrils. How she hated that odor; how it reminded her of his rancid, whiskey breath and that cold night only a month past. . . .

Something moved again in the woods, something shadowy and instantly terrifying. It brought a flood of emotion and memories of that night, reminded her what evil could lurk beneath the frigid autumn moon.

Whatever prowled in the woodland moved slowly, stalking her like a mountain cat set to pounce on an elk, but she refused to let her terror make her easy prey, the way it had before.

Whirling, she ran, muscles stiff and gait clumsy. She nearly tripped over a section of branch that had fallen onto the trail. Ankle twisting, pain ripped through her calf and foot. Tears flooded her eyes, though she wasn't completely certain they weren't more from fright than pain.

She stumbled onward. She couldn't let pain stop her, couldn't let whoever was out there gain an inch of ground.

A sudden crashing came from the woods diagonally to her left, roughly ten feet back. Someone *was* there, someone gaining on her.

'Please, God, don't let it happen again . . .' Her words

came in stuttered gasps. Her lungs burned. Her heart pounded so severely she swore it would burst through her ribcage. Memories swept before her mind again, flashes of images – his face, his hands, his smug expression as he—

She let out a bleat as her toe hooked a rut in the hard-pack. She plunged forward, thrusting her arms out before her. Agony tore through her palms as they contacted the ground and flesh scraped against pebbles and frost-hardened soil.

Her arms buckled and she came down on elbows and forearms. Her torso impacted a second later; air exploded from her lungs and stars burst across her vision.

She lay there, stunned, unsure whether she had blacked out, because suddenly she was gasping and staring straight ahead at the trail, as if a curtain had whisked up.

Tears flooded her eyes again but she refused to let them flow. *Get up*, she told herself. *You have to go on. You can't give up.*

She pushed herself up into a sitting position, palms singing with pain and skin scraped off various places all the way to her elbows. Her blouse had torn along one side, exposing the chemise beneath.

Fear filled her with strength. Blood rushed through her veins, hot with adrenaline. Her legs quivered as she rose to her feet, casting a sweeping glance along the woods to her side, then behind her.

Quiet. The shushing of the breeze fondling the leaves, the shimmering of shadows coupling with dirty-amber moonlight.

Her heart pounded in her ears; her pulse throbbed in her temples. She shuddered, fearing she would shake loose from her bones and fall back to the ground. Only her terror-filled memories of a month before held her up.

Emptiness loomed behind her. No one sprang from the woods, nothing moved now. Had she imagined it? Had terror gotten the better of her nerves and rendered her rational mind incapable of distinguishing the difference between nightmare and reality?

Maybe it was some animal after all, a bear, a cougar.

Wrapping her paining arms about herself, lips quivering, she uttered a silent prayer and decided to hell with the man who was supposed to meet her. Let him meet up with whatever was out there in the woods. He damn well took his chances in his line of work.

She turned, intending to run for home and never look back.

Instead, she froze. A wave of ice washed through her body until suddenly she could no longer feel her legs. A scream died in her throat and her head reeled again, the trail swinging in an arc before her vision. She was going to lose consciousness and that would be the end. She would be vulnerable again, and this time she knew she would never live through it.

A man stood there, unmoving, leaning against a tree, eyes narrowed and somehow glimmering in the dusky light. His face appeared pale, soft-featured, yet at the same time held a measure of viciousness she'd seldom witnessed on a human being.

The man chuckled, a sound that held no hint of humor. He pulled a silver case from his shirt pocket beneath his dark coat, then flicked it open. Selecting a cigarette he poked it between thin lips and returned the case to his pocket, then fished out a lucifer and struck it against the bark of the tree. The match flared, illuminating his face with warmer glow for an instant, though it softened his features not at all. Pinpoints of light reflected in blue eyes that appeared unfathomably cruel.

She drew a stuttering breath, fighting off the sensation of fainting. Confronting the cause of her terror made it somehow easier.

The man lit the cigarette and drew a deep drag, blowing out an exaggerated cloud of smoke mixed with breath steam.

'Evenin'.' His voice came utterly flat, yet more chilled than the night air.

'Y-you . . . you were followin' me? In the woods?' Her words came stammering, quaking, tongue refusing to work right. She fought to keep on her feet, force her heart to stop pounding.

'That wouldn't be the gentlemanly thing to do, now would it, missy?' A hint of a smile took his thin lips, but the expression proved in no way comforting or warm. Here was a man devoid of human compassion, she thought. Here was a man of death.

He was lying. She could see it in his eyes. Men were open books to her; she could always read them, knew what they were thinkin', sometimes before they thought it. Her mother had been part gypsy and she reckoned it came from that. This man was no different, just emptier.

Her face tightened. 'It *was* you. Don't lie to me.'

He laughed, a crisp gibbering thing that danced over the brisk autumn air and dissolved as quickly as it came.

'Well, missy, never did claim I was a gentleman, now, did I?'

She bit her lower lip to stop it from quivering. Her legs shook, but she felt stronger, less likely to pass out.

'Just who are you?'

He stared at her, something predatory in the look. His gaze slithered down her body, lingering at the fullness of her breasts, then roved over her skirt and back up. A note of appreciation mixed with the filthiness of the look, repulsing her, replacing some of the fright with disgust.

'Why, missy, I'm your huckleberry.' He took another drag on the cigarette and snapped the smoke out in purse-lipped blow.

She couldn't stop another chill from shuddering through her, though she had guessed the answer before he gave it.

'You're Lacy?'

He nodded curtly and tipped a finger to the brim of his creased Stetson. Long thin fingers on a soft-looking, thin-skinned hand. Stringy veins wriggled across its surface like slate-colored worms.

'I'm Lacy. At your service – Miss Barton, is it?'

She uttered a whispered, 'Yes', and her gaze flicked away, unable to hold his cold stare. 'I don't require your services any more, sir. Please . . . go back where you came from.' Her gaze shifted back to his. She absently brushed errant strands of auburn hair away from her forehead, then tucked them back beneath the powder-blue kerchief she wore.

His face tightened a notch and she realized he was younger than she had first thought, hardly more than a boy, really, twenty or twenty-one at the most. For the briefest of instances a strange sadness welled inside her, like something a mother might feel for a child gone wrong. Fear rushed back in, chasing the sadness away, as she remembered just what this man was: a killer. He murdered men in cold blood and accepted payment for the deed. He was no boy, no mother's child, at least not any longer. He was an instrument of death, a soulless man-child.

And she was little better than that for summoning him here.

After a moment of frozen silence Lacy took another drag on the cigarette, then tossed it to the ground.

'Reckon I didn't hear you correct, missy.' His eyes narrowed.

'Indeed, you heard me correct, sir. I made a mistake sending for you. I realize that now. I was distraught, not thinking right. Please accept my apologies for your inconvenience.' Her voice shook and she reckoned not a lick of her speech was dissuading.

He pushed himself away from the tree, took a step towards her.

'Who gave you my name, missy?'

Her breath clutched and she didn't want to stay in his presence a moment longer. She wanted to run, lock herself in her home and pray the boyish killer would ride back to where he came from.

'I done asked you a question.' The man's voice lowered, carrying a blatant threat. 'You best answer it.' He took another step, dried, frost-glazed leaves crackling beneath his boots.

She pushed out her chin, steadied her voice.

'You know his name, sir. He contacted you.'

'That don't make no difference. I asked *you* to tell me.'

She didn't care for the way his tone belittled her, like a cruel parent preparing to switch a child within an inch of his life. But fright compelled her to answer him.

'Sutter was his name. Drunk in town. Told me you were

the best at . . . at what you do.'

'He's right.' His smile got wider, snakelike. 'He tell you once an order's placed ain't no goin' back on it? He tell you I don't give refunds?'

She shook her head. 'No, sir, he did not. But I have your money.' She reached into her pocket and pulled loose the folded bills, held them out to him at arm's length. Her hand shook violently and the man chuckled, obviously taking pleasure from her fear. 'Please, just take it and go away. Don't do the job, I beg you. The money's yours, free and clear.'

He gazed at the cash, running his tongue over his front teeth.

'Reckon you don't make that much as a schoolmarm and dressmaker. Must have taken a spell to save up those greenbacks.'

A note of surprise escaped her lips and something in her belly plunged.

'How do you know that? I told you nothing about myself in the telegram.'

He laughed, taking another step closer.

'I know all about you, missy. Make it a point never to ride in blind when a client hires me. Too many lawmen smart enough to try a ruse.'

'Just take the money and leave me be. Please. You can't go through with what I wanted. I wasn't in my right mind when I called on you.' She tossed the folded cash to the hardpack in front of his feet.

He gazed down, then knelt and plucked the money from the ground. Stuffing it into a pocket, he straightened, cold eyes settling on her. A lascivious glint sparkled within them.

'Don't intend to go through with it . . .' His voice came out a whisper.

Somewhere a horse nickered and her gaze swept past him. She spotted the animal twenty feet down the trail, tethered to a tree. His horse. He'd been stalking her all along, watching, making certain she was alone and vulnerable. It came to her suddenly. He was here for more than just the job and her money, though he would steal her long-saved earnings as well. He was here on behalf of the very man upon whom she'd sought revenge.

The notion galvanizing her, she made a mad dash into the forest at trailside. Blind fear and survival instinct filled her legs with strength. She prayed she could somehow lose him in terrain unfamiliar to him.

He leaped after her, animal-like, with liquid movement. The sound of his steps behind her were no longer crashing and clumsy. He had no wish to frighten her with some cat-and-mouse game now; he wanted to catch her, finish what he had come to do.

She swept through fir-boughs, the needles tearing at her skirt and blouse, swiping her face. Her feet rolled on fallen branches lurking beneath the thick underbrush, nearly sending her to the ground times over.

Her heart banged with renewed force, throbbing in her throat. Her breath beat out, hot and shallow. She prayed she could outrun him, somehow reach her cabin, where she had a Winchester.

Chancing a backward look, she saw his hurtling form, a mere ten feet behind. He maneuvered through the brush far better than she had hoped.

'Give it up, missy!' His yell carried a ghostly quality in

the frigid night, wholly chilling. 'I'll be right sweet to you, I promise.'

Lying again. The man had likely never said a truthful word in his life, she reckoned, and she knew now she had made an even bigger mistake sending for him than she first thought. He had come not to accomplish the job she hired him for, but to strike her like the lightning of righteousness for daring to take life and death into her own hands. It was too late to beg for forgiveness, too late to atone.

Her head swiveled forward, just in time to avoid running straight into a thick spruce. She twisted, boughs tearing at her as she thrust her arms out before her to sweep them away. Smashing into the boughs spun her half-around, sending her stumbling diagonally into the bole of a huge maple. She hit hard, rebounding from the tree, nearly losing consciousness. Shadow and amber swirled before her vision. She wasn't certain what kept her on her feet, careening forward through the woodland. Her body acted as if of its own accord.

The night forest reeled before her. Sounds of him running through brush penetrated her dazed mind again and snapped her senses back to reality.

Closer, now. Too close. She swore she could feel his hot breath beating on the back of her neck, swore she could feel his fingers reaching out for her—

Her foot caught in a rabbit hole and sharp pain skewered her ankle as it twisted left and her body jerked right.

Falling. An exaggerated dream-motion. Brush thrust into her face, scratching. Her body slammed against the forest floor. Breath exploded from her lungs. Gasping, she instantly jerked her foot free of the hole, but it was too late.

She twisted onto her back to see him standing over her,

breathing hard and no longer smiling. His features, marbled with shadow and amber moonlight, appeared demonic, condemning.

'I told you no refunds, missy. Reckon it's time you got something for your money.'

He bent, making a grab for her. She let out a short scream and thrust her leg out in a snapping kick to his shin.

Pain lanced his features. 'Christ, woman!' He stumbled back a step, blistering the chilly air with a string of curses.

She wasted no time surveying her work. Scuttling backwards, she twisted and jumped to her feet. Her ankle screamed with pain; her heart thudded so hard she thought it would explode from her chest.

She tried to run, but he recovered too fast and leaped after her. His girlish hands grabbed at her blouse, snatching up handfuls and spinning her around. She came face to face with him, stared into those cold blue eyes. Empty, empty as the Devil's, was all she could think.

Uttering a chopped scream, she raked his face with her fingernails, determined she would never let another man take what she didn't offer.

Releasing his hold, he let out a bleat of pain and backhanded her.

She staggered, the gunmetal taste of her own blood filling her mouth, legs threatening to go in opposite directions. Pain radiated through her teeth and blood ribboned from her lips.

He grabbed at her again and instinct compelled her to fight back. She swung fists at him, kicked viciously at his kneecaps. He managed to avoid most of the blows by seizing her arms and shaking her. His small frame concealed more power than she expected.

Jerking up a knee, she sought to plant it squarely where it would do the most damage. He twisted at the last second, but took enough of the blow to make his face contort and air burst from his lungs. He groaned, grip slackening an instant.

She tore away from him. Hurling herself backward, she intended to spin and make a final attempt to flee for her house, but her legs tangled in her skirt and her feet swept out from beneath her. She went down, hitting the ground hard on her left side. Tiny grunts of pain came to her lips as she tried to drag herself forward, escape his hands, which clawed at her legs. He grabbed both of her ankles, fingers digging in, sending spikes of agony through her legs. Jerking hard, he dragged her back and turned her over on to her back.

She tried to kick loose from his grip, but he held her ankles fast.

Strong, too strong, her panicked mind responded. She curled forward, one hand grasping his trousers leg, the other balling into a fist. She buried her knuckles with as much force as she could muster into his crotch. Lacy's face went purple and he coughed a burst of air and spittle. He released her ankles, then doubled, groaning.

She thrust herself backward by kicking her heels against the hard ground.

She couldn't reach her feet fast enough.

Lacy recovered more quickly than she imagined any man ever being capable of. He pounced on her, snatching up two handfuls of her blouse, then hoisting her to her feet. Fabric ripped, exposing more of the chemise.

He flung her sideways and she collided with an aspen.

The impact stunned her nearly senseless. She started to crumple, but he grabbed her again, whirled her around like a feather caught in a cyclone, flung her left. She flew over a deadfall, landing square in a patch of brush that cushioned her fall not in the least. Burrs punctured her skirt and bit at her legs. She gasped for air, fighting a wave of blackness that threatened to consume her senses. Her forearms and hands bled and auburn hair hung disheveled about her face, torn loose from the kerchief now lying in the brush next to her.

He pounced again, grasping handfuls of her blouse and hoisting her to her feet. She dazedly peered into his eyes, saw no mercy there, no remorse, only perverse pleasure. He enjoyed hurting folks, enjoyed hurting those weaker than himself.

He let go of one handful of material, backhanded her. The blow collided with her jaw, snapped her head back. Stars flared and perished before her vision. Pain rang distantly now. Her legs buckled and she tipped backwards. With his grip retained by only one fistful of her blouse he couldn't stop her fall. The fabric tore, most of the blouse front ripping loose in his hand.

He flung it aside and jumped after her, coming down atop her as she lay flat on her back. Her thoughts spun, one moment thankful for the thin chemise between him and her soft flesh, the next swollen with terror at the notion he would be able to do whatever he damn well wanted with her now and she would never be able to resist. She couldn't even lift her arms to fight him off. Her muscles felt leaden, powerless.

A glint of moonlight flashed from something suddenly in his hand—

No, oh, God, no! I don't want to die . . .

A gun. A gun that somehow looked miles long before her fright-widened eyes. He jammed the bore against her lips, which she pressed tightly together, barely able to breath through her bloodied nose. He laughed, clacking her with the barrel, splitting her lower lip.

Her mouth opened involuntarily and he shoved the Smith & Wesson between her teeth. A chilled numbness washed over her. She couldn't move, couldn't even twitch. She was going to die and she had no one to blame but herself.

Lacy leaned in closer, wiggling the barrel against her teeth, causing splinters of pain. His expression showed more emotion now, a perverse ecstasy.

'Case you ain't figured it out yet, missy, I don't take my work lightly. You called me, I came, but unlucky for you someone else could afford to pay me a hell of a lot more or your job might already be done and you wouldn't be starin' up at the wrong end of my Smithy. Fact, I would have taken your money, then shot you dead. Only reason you're still breathin' is acause I make more money by not buryin' you. 'Course, if you was to die alone out here, that'd hardly be my fault, now, would it?'

He stared into her eyes for what seemed an eternity, then slowly withdrew the barrel from her mouth. Sliding the Smith & Wesson into its holster at his hip, he backed off her. For a moment he stood staring down at her shuddering frame. With a thin laugh, he turned and walked away. She heard him crashing through the brush, but the sounds of his passage soon faded. A few moments later, the clopping of hoofs receded into the distance.

He had left her alive, hadn't taken from her what the

other had a month before. At once she was overcome with joy for her second chance at life, yet stricken with terror because Lacy's leaving her this way was meant as a warning, and she knew from whom. Only one man around these parts was rich enough to pay off Lacy. The message was plain: never attempt anything so foolish as getting even again.

She had lost it all now. Her dignity and any chance at scrubbing the stain from her soul, her money.

Tears rushed into her eyes. She sat up, sobbing with her face in her hands for long minutes.

When she eventually managed to stand, she could barely keep her balance. Her muscles trembled and pain rang from every area of her body. She spat a stream of blood and saliva, then stumbled forward, sweeping aside branches and boughs, nearly going down numerous times. Her lungs burned and weakness increased the more she walked. She would never make it home. Lacy had spared her only so she could die on the trail.

She staggered out of the woods onto the hardpack, the last of her strength deserting her legs. She collapsed, pitching forward. She got her arms out in front of her but they helped little to blunt the impact. Her face hit the ground and she lay there, panting, pain the only thing keeping her mercilessly conscious.

A sound. Pounding in her ears, vibrating through the hardpack beneath her cheek.

Hoofs. Had Lacy come back to finish the job?

She lifted her head as the sound came to a stop. Blood snaked from the corner of her mouth. She struggled to focus.

No, not Lacy. A dark angel. Damn, she was dying after

all, because here he was, sitting atop a bay horse staring down at her: the Angel of Death.

'Help me . . .' she managed to whisper, unsure why she should be asking the Angel of Death for assistance. Maybe it was because death would bring comfort and peace at last from the night that haunted her. Maybe it was because it would end the pain and humiliation in her heart.

Maybe it was because she had just given up.

CHAPTER TWO

John Deletéreo stared out through the small window, brown eyes scanning the moonlit grounds for any sign of the man who had battered the young woman lying on the sofa behind him. The moon had turned from blood to alabaster and gleamed a hand's-span above the trees rimming the property a hundred yards distant. Shadows shifted and ghostly light painted the frost-varnished grass. Nothing human moved, nothing threatened, though the eerie shivering black and white landscape unearthed a foreboding sense of menace somewhere deep within him. He'd stumbled into something, something dark and dangerous; he had felt the chilled specter of Fate brush past him.

It wasn't the first time.

A sigh parted his lips. He hadn't ridden to Payton's Bluff to become involved in the locals' troubles. But troubles had a way of seeking him out. He reckoned he was some sort of magnet for others' misfortune, though Lord knew he'd been dealt enough of his own.

What could he do? Wouldn't have been right to leave her lying there hurt on the trail. She never would have survived the night.

Some claimed John Deletéreo no longer possessed any compassion, but that wasn't entirely true. It just depended on who was seeking it from him, devil or angel. He had very little middle ground; Clarissa had always considered that a fault in him, and maybe she had been right. He saw things in stark black and white, rarely in shades. It was the one certainty he accepted in himself, the one part he hadn't come to this place to find.

Truth be told, compromise mattered even less to him now. What value had such a trait to a man who died two years back?

He clenched his teeth, muscles rippling to either side of his angular jaw, and forced memories of Clarissa back into the corner of his memory where they could not dredge pain from his heart. She was gone; no use reliving the past in his mind; bad enough nightmares replayed that day without mercy.

Water droplets trickled down the windowpane and as his focus tightened he saw his face reflected in the glass. His gloved fingers went to the scar on his left cheek and dark grief threatened to surge up and bring tears to his soul. His eyelids fluttered closed. Opening them again, he forced a deep breath, struggling to repel the assault of memories. For an instant his face dissolved in the glass and Clarissa's soft features stared back at him, pleading, blood-drenched. He reached for her . . .

Touched only a thin, chilled pane. He shuddered, blinked. Gone. She was gone. Only his face remained frozen in the glass, only his bewildered stare.

No one would have called John Deletéreo an old man – in fact his twenty-fifth birthday had passed without much notice on his part three weeks past – but life and the elements had welded years to his face, scrawling deep lines into his forehead and tarnishing his brown eyes with melancholy. His complexion hinted at his half-Mex heritage and wavy dark hair fell just past his ears. As he turned from the window his dark gray duster swept back to reveal black trousers riveted with silver studs that ran along the outside of either leg down to his boots. The ivory handle of a Colt Peacemaker, upon which was carved a skull, flashed into view, but he quickly pulled the coat flap over it. No need to alarm the woman when she regained consciousness. A black Stetson rested atop his head.

He tugged off his gloves and tucked them into the duster's right pocket. Leaning against the wall beside the window, he folded his arms across his chest, which was covered with a black hide shirt laced with leather down to the sternum.

His gaze roved about the room. The home was small, consisting of two rooms, a parlor and kitchen. Clapboard sided the exterior and even in the poor lighting he'd noticed spots in need of repair. He'd glimpsed a small garden to the right of the place, an empty corral with sagging fences to the left.

The home's interior was cluttered, but well kept. He judged from an entire corner of the room taken up by bolts of calico and wool, along with piles of canvas from wagon tops, buckskin and buffalo hide, that the woman was a dressmaker. A loom stood close to the materials and he spotted bins labeled goldenrod, walnut bark, sumac and butternut hulls, all of which garment-makers used for coloring cloth. A number of books stacked in two piles rested on a small table, so perhaps she provided learning for children, or tutored. Beside the stacks lay copies of *Harper's Bazaar* and *Godey's Lady's Book*. Above the table, on wall pegs, rested a Winchester.

On a second table near the sofa sat a lantern, high flame casting a bright buttery glow. Two more lanterns adorned the walls, illuminating the corners, flames turned higher than need be. He wondered if she feared the shadows, and whether it had anything to do with whoever had attacked her on the trail tonight.

The woman had been lucky he'd been riding towards town when he was, or she might well have died out there on that trail. Although her injuries weren't as serious as they appeared at first glance, she would have been prey to any number of forest beasts, or perished from exposure, seeing as how she was dressed only in a thin skirt and chemise and the temperature would plunge even further by dawnfall.

He went to the couch where she lay, watching her a moment as she muttered something in her sleep. She'd regain consciousness in a few minutes, he reckoned.

Kneeling, he pulled the bandanna loose from his neck and dipped it into a bucket beside the sofa. He had taken the liberty of fetching water from the pump to the left of the house, then boiling it in a kettle he found resting on the cast-iron stove in the kitchen. It had cooled enough for use.

He gently dabbed at the dried blood and welts on her face, with his free hand sweeping back strands of auburn hair from her forehead. Despite the beating, she had a gentle loveliness. Not what most folks would call beautiful in the fashion of one of them fancy ladies he had met in New York, but a natural comeliness that went deeper than skin. She reminded him of Clarissa in that way.

Stinging grief came with the thought and he forced his attention away from the woman's looks. He finished cleaning the blood from her lips and nostrils and draped the bandanna over the edge of the bucket.

Her eyelids blinked open and she started. Pushing herself back against the sofa, she stared at him, wide-eyed. He couldn't recollect seeing such fear in a woman's eyes before. And pain. Some deep pain that went beyond whatever happened to her tonight. He recognized the signs only too well; he had seen them staring back at him from the mirror too many times not to: the loss of something precious, something that could never be returned.

'Easy, ma'am.' He straightened and backed off a couple steps.

'W-who are you?' Her voice quivered. 'Are you Death?'

It struck him as a damned peculiar question, though maybe not entirely inaccurate. He reckoned she was still stunned, in her mind perhaps still back there on the trail.

'I found you lying on the trail. Brought you back here after you told me about this place. You passed out after.' He tried to make his voice reassuring, comforting, but truth was he hadn't much practice at that sort of thing over the past two years, so it fell short of the mark.

She searched his face, as if trying to read every line, every nuance, for lies. Some of the fear receded and she looked less dazed. She took a long breath.

'I recollect, now. I thought . . . I thought you were the Angel of Death.'

A thin smile creased his lips. 'Been called worse, I reckon. Who did this to you?' His brown eyes locked with hers, the prettiest shade of amethyst he'd ever seen. She looked away, and her face went a shade paler.

'I . . . I don't know. It was dark.'

She was lying. He heard it in the hitch in her voice, saw it in the manner in which she fidgeted after she got herself into a sitting position.

He went back to the window, glanced out, then back to her.

'You must have seen someone, ma'am. Moon's almost full.'

She glanced at him, a guilty expression flicking across her features.

'What I meant was, I didn't see his face. He was wearing a mask.'

Still lying, but he couldn't force her into telling him.

'How was he dressed? Big fella or little?'

'Big, I think. Yes, he was big, strong. Dark clothes.' She stared at a spot on the floor and her fingers went to her swollen lips, probing gingerly. He noticed her hand trembled.

Folding his arms, he glanced back out the window, watching the shadows sway.

'Where'd he come from? Ridin' a horse of any particular breed or color?' He looked back at her with a slight frown.

Her gaze rose to meet his, a note of defiance sparking within her eyes.

'What does it matter? He's gone now.'

He shrugged, the frown deepening.

'I'm headin' into town. I could fetch the marshal and have him go after this fella before he hurts you again.'

She let out a low laugh, but quickly covered it.

'No . . . no, that won't be necessary. I'm sure he was just someone passing through. Reckon he won't be back.'

Something in her voice told him she was worried about that very thing, the man returning to finish the job he'd started. He got the strong notion the attack had far more behind it than she chose to reveal.

'You know any reason he would attack you? He take anything?'

'Money . . . he took some money I had in my pocket. I reckon that's all he was after. Just some highwayman passing through. I put up a fight, so he beat me. It's my own fault.' She averted her eyes again, and he caught a peculiar inflection on her last sentence, but couldn't pinpoint the meaning behind it. He felt certain she'd lied again, though not from some malicious attempt to deceive but from deep fear. The backstory, whatever it was, intrigued him. *She* intrigued him. But he hadn't ridden to Payton's Bluff for mystery and if she didn't want to tell him, that was her right. No point pressing the issue.

'Reckon you might be right.' His tone lowered. 'Best you inform the marshal, though. Just in case that fella takes a notion to come back here and raid your place.'

She nodded. 'I'll do that, mister. First thing tomorrow morning.'

A thin smile touched his lips. She wouldn't tell the marshal, not tomorrow, not ever. He saw it plain on her face and it only made him more curious about whatever she was involved in.

He decided to change the subject, relax her a bit. Maybe she'd trust him more then.

'You a dressmaker?'

She nodded, shifting and wincing, then wrapping her arms about herself, as if she'd just realized she wore only a thin chemise.

'I sell to a catalog back East. Some fancy ladies buy my dresses.'

'The books?' He ducked his chin to the table.

'I teach at the school . . . least I used to. School got out for harvest season but town replaced me anyway, so I won't be going back to it.' The pain returned to her eyes.

'Why'd they do that?'

Her face reddened and small lines creased her brow.

'Reckon I don't see how that's any of your business, Mr – I don't even know your name.'

'John. My name's John.'

She raised an eyebrow. 'Got a last name?'

He nodded. 'Anyhow, was just makin' conversation. I best be headin' to town now.'

She tensed visibly and came to her feet, still keeping her arms across her breasts.

'Why you headin' into Payton's Bluff?' Her voice had that hitch again, though this time it came from something other than deception; worry, maybe, though he couldn't guess why.

To find myself, he felt like answering, but repressed the urge.

'I got business there, I reckon. Least someone told me I do.'

'Who told you?'

He gave her a smile touched with sarcasm.

'Now who's askin' questions none of their business?'

Her eyes narrowed and tiny flames ignited. She didn't care a lick for her words being thrown back at her.

'Payton's Bluff's a rathole, mister. You'd best ride the other way and not look back.' Her tone grew serious now, laced with a measure of concern.

'Reckon a rathole's the best place to go if you're huntin' rats.'

She cocked an eyebrow, holding herself tighter.

'What does that mean?'

He shrugged, stepped away from the window.

'Nothing, I reckon. It means nothing. I best be goin'. You might want to see the doc tomorrow. Don't think you got any broken bones, but couldn't hurt to have an expert take a look.'

Her lips pressed into a tight line and she gave a curt nod.

He tipped his finger to his hat and went to the door.

'Mister?' she said behind him.

He turned to her, hand on the door handle.

'Yes, ma'am?'

She stared a moment, then shook her head.

'Just . . . just watch yourself in that town, is all. Some bad folks there.'

'I'll keep that in mind, ma'am.' He paused. 'Don't believe I ever got your name.'

She almost smiled. 'Kylie Barton.'

'Don't go walkin' along trails at night alone, Kylie Barton. Never know what's out there.' With that he stepped out into the night.

Kylie went to the window and watched the man mount his bay, swing the animal around and heel it into a walk. He appeared in no particular hurry and she could see him peering about, as if making certain no one lurked close by. The notion made her feel safer somehow, and something about the man had struck her as kind, maybe even concerned. Hard to figure from a man, especially the sort she'd come in contact with of late.

Although she thanked her Maker that no bones were broken and nothing more than her pride was permanently bruised, every corner of her body pained and disgust turned in her belly. Stupid, that's what she had been. Plumb stupid. She was lucky to be alive – if she could call spending more days with the burden of her nightmare truly living.

Perhaps she would have been better off had that Lacy fella killed her. What did she have now to look forward to anyway? A life filled with the scorn of that no-good town, jeers and ridicule? To be forever branded a liar? She had prided herself on her word, her honor. And one man had taken all that from her.

Now, to make matters worse, she had compounded all that by losing all her savings to a killer.

'Go to the marshal,' that man riding away had told her. What a laugh that would be. What would she tell Studdard – that she had hired someone to kill a no-good bastard no one in town would dare say a condescending word to? The son of the richest cattleman in this part of Colorado Territory? The marshal would sooner throw her in a cell and hang her with the sunrise than lift a finger against a Galendez.

The worthless lawdog knew the truth about what happened last month. He *knew*. But he didn't care. And he wouldn't listen to anything she had to say now. No one would. For all she knew, he'd give that weasel Lacy a free hand at her and turn his back.

A caged feeling washed over her, as if the familiar walls of her home suddenly trapped her now, her sanctuary alien, no longer providing the security she always thought she would have. Things just hadn't been the same since Cole was killed in that mining accident three years back. A young bride suddenly left to her own, even with an established client list as a dressmaker, was no better than an unweaned babe when it came to making her way in the untamed West. She had thought she was so damnably strong, so able, but all that was a lie, an illusion that melted in the harsh light of reality. These past three years had been so hard for her, every day filled with loneliness and questions about the worth of going on living, every night plagued with hopelessness and worry. Last month made it so much worse, and now she saw things as a downward spiral, a constant struggle to survive another sunrise in the unfeeling, loathsome hell that was Payton's Bluff.

She could move, relocate some place far from this God-forsaken hole, in fact had planned on it. That was what she had been saving for until she got it into her fool head to hire that Lacy fella. Now, even that chance was gone. Maybe just as well. She'd never outrun the memories, the filth one man's wanton hunger had affixed to her soul.

A tear slipped from her eye. Damn, she refused to cry over it, but couldn't stop herself.

Coming from her black thoughts, she watched the man named John receding into the distance, as he headed for the trail. Something about him . . .

Pain. She saw pain within him, though he tried to hide it. But other things, too, things she couldn't fathom. Had she even lost her ability to read men now? Had the gypsy in her perished with the beating Lacy administered? Or had an uncaring God taken the last of her gifts from her?

Maybe. Or maybe he was just an enigma. She caught

herself wishing he would return, and it surprised her. She didn't truly know the man, though he had been gallant enough to bring her back here and treat her kindly. She reckoned she should have been more leery after Ty Galendez, suspicious of every man, now, and in fact she reckoned she was when it came down to it. But this man John . . . he was different. Somehow.

Who was he? A stranger to her, but she had caught a glimpse of the gun beneath his duster, had seen the confident way he carried himself and the lines and small scar on his face that hinted at a harsh life. Conflicting signs and impressions. Unlike any man she'd met before, even her late husband, a sturdy solid man who knew little about showing affection but everything about providing for a family. A family that never came to be.

The tears welled again and she swept her hand across her cheek, brushing them away.

She watched the man disappear into the night, wondering if she would ever see him again, feeling a certain melancholy because she doubted she would.

Returning to the sofa, she curled her legs to her chest, wrapped her arms about her knees and remained awake for the remainder of the night, afraid to sleep, afraid to dream, afraid to hope.

CHAPTER THREE

Kylie Barton.

The name lingered in John Deletéreo's mind as he rode the trail towards Payton's Bluff. She had lied outright to him, yet a strong desire to help her made him want to turn around and ride back to her homestead. He cursed that desire. Tangling himself in a deceitful woman's troubles was probably the last thing he needed to distract him from his purpose here.

Chilly air whipped at his face, rouging his cheeks, as he heeled the bay into a faster gait. The cold penetrated to his bones, stung his hands.

Questions lingered in his mind. Who had attacked a defenseless woman and why? Was the assault and robbery the work of a passing-through highwayman, the motive simple robbery – or something more complicated? Why beat her, yet leave her alive to tell the tale? Why not simply kill her and hide her body in the forest? No one would have found it for days, if ever.

Granted, the attacker might have figured on her dying from her injuries or exposure, but that meant risking a posse on his tail if she somehow survived. The bandit surely would have been smarter making sure she never talked.

Unless he was someone known to her, someone she wouldn't dare point a finger at . . .

He didn't care for that suspicion, though it fitted pieces together in a readable pattern.

Maybe she was simply too frightened to trust him. He reckoned he couldn't blame her and it painted a better image than a woman mixed up in criminal activity. He was a stranger, after all; likely she was leery of anyone offering to help after such a brutal attack.

It didn't explain her reluctance to fetch the marshal, though, did it?

That was a question he intended to answer directly and in short order. It might delay his quest in Payton's Bluff, but maybe he was more hesitant about learning the facts on that account than he cared to admit. Maybe the woman's plight provided just the excuse he needed to avoid a painful truth a few more hours.

The truth about a man named John Deletéreo.

The West's most dangerous manhunter. That's what the damn pulp novels said. That label had saddled him with a passel of grief, nightmares he continually relived.

Johnny Dead. A nickname tagged to him at the whim of some faceless author. An avenger who showed no remorse killing those who deserved it, then vanished like a ghost in the night.

A dead man.

To a large extent he reckoned the reputation was justified. But only since Clarissa's death. Before that, cheap words on grainy paper. That writer had fashioned Johnny Dead from whole cloth; now John Deletéreo lived the reality.

Who was he?

How many times over the past two weeks had he asked himself that question? A hundred? A thousand? Too many to count. Who was he, indeed. A mythical specter defending the innocent? A killer? A man without a heritage or identity?

He had journeyed to Payton's Bluff for just that answer; somewhere in the depths of his soul it frightened him to know he would not leave without learning it.

The woman was right: Payton's Bluff was a rathole. Riding in, he slowed his mount to a walk. Despite the chill of the night, men staggered about the street and boardwalks, some fighting, others vomiting over rails. Shouts and raucous laughter rang out from the saloon. A tinkler piano-player pounded on the keys, producing an disharmonic jangle. A soiled dove posed outside the saloon entrance, dressed in a purple sateen bodice that plumped her assets into twin mounds of gooseflesh. Left leg bent, skirt-covered heel braced against the clapboard siding, she cast him a suggestive look and let splayed fingers drift just below her belly. He shook his head and she raised her hand in an unladylike gesture, spat, then disappeared into the drinkerie.

A gunshot thundered from somewhere, but no one paid it any mind.

A cowboy urinated in the open, directing his aim at another fella passed out in the street next to the boardwalk.

Payton's Bluff was laid out in a rough Y shape punctuated by numerous dark alleys and cross streets. Hanging lanterns flickered buttery puddles across the wide rutted street and garbage scuttled along the boardwalks, driven by a blue breeze. He spotted various businesses – mercantile, café, general store, gunshop – and, a bit farther down, the marshal's office. A light burned within.

A haven for cowboys blowing off steam after the day's ranch duties, for women of the line lusting after fat wallets and easy marks, and likely for every despot passing through. He'd seen countless towns of such ilk, and like all the rest this one brought the same measure of disgust to his belly. Just the place he'd expected to unearth his pedigree.

The air carried the stench of urine, stale vomit, horse dung and rotted food. His nostrils twitched and his stomach rebelled, but he reckoned he'd get used to it after a spell.

He reined up just before the marshal's office and dismounted. He tethered his horse to the hitch rail, then stepped onto the boards and started towards the door, alert for bandits concealed in the shadows. Towns like this, a fella was lucky to keep his money and his life intact.

Two men staggered from an alley a few yards behind him. Blood spackled their faces and each appeared intent on doing his damnedest to pound the other senseless. Entangled, they stumbled across the boardwalk, slammed into the rail. Wood split with a tremendous snap as they plunged through. They crashed down in the street. The fellow on top, features pinpointing him as a hardcase, balled a fist and proceeded to hammer the man beneath him. He would kill his victim in short order.

John stepped towards them, letting out a sharp 'Hey!'

The hardcase looked up, eyes gleaming with viciousness. These weren't drunks, that became instantly obvious.

The man on top was an outlaw but the one suffering the most damage looked like a regular cowhand.

'Get the hell outa here, fella.' The hardcase's tone carried a clear threat. 'This ain't none of your concern.' He stood, leaving his victim groaning and bleeding in the dust.

'Leave him be.' John's tone lowered a notch, grew as chilled as the night air.

The hardcase peered at him, steam coming from his mouth as he panted, hate glaring from his eyes.

'Who the hell you think you are, stranger?' The outlaw closed the distance between them, hand moving towards the gun at his belt.

In a blur of movement, the Peacemaker filled John's hand. His arm snapped straight out, jamming the barrel against the man's lumpy brow.

Likely the hardcase had never witnessed a draw quite so fast. His expression flashed into a mask of shock. His hand stopped in mid-motion.

'Maybe a third eye would help you see things better?' John asked without a hint of humor.

The hardcase licked his lips, rolled his gaze towards the barrel pressed to his forehead.

'Reckon that ain't necessary.' The threat had vanished from his tone.

'Best we don't meet again.'

The man nodded, then whirled and ran. He didn't stop running until he disappeared at the far end of town.

John holstered his Peacemaker and stepped over to the fallen man. He offered a hand as the cowhand pushed himself into a sitting position and glared.

'What the hell right you got stickin' your nose in?' The

man's words came with a harsh reprimand, and no hint of gratitude for having just had his life spared. He spat at John's hand, scrambled to his feet, then staggered off towards the saloon. John stared after him, wiping his hand on his trousers. He should have let them kill each other, he reckoned.

He turned and went towards the marshal's office. A rangy man with ropy muscles looked up at him from behind a desk as he entered and closed the door behind him.

He doffed his Stetson, approached the desk.

'What the hell do you want?' The marshal held a pulp novel and an annoyed expression. John noticed a slight glaze to the lawdog's eyes and a half-empty whiskey glass on the desk.

'Hell of a town you got here, Marshal.' John ducked his chin towards the door.

'So? You ride in for a tour or there some order of business you got in mind?'

'Came to report a crime.' He refused to let the man's abrasive manner put him off.

'That so?' The marshal swung his feet off the desk and closed his pulp novel, setting it on the blotter. The lines of annoyance on his face deepened.

'Woman was attacked on the trail leading into your town. Thought you might be interested in knowing about it.'

The marshal cocked an eyebrow.

'What woman?'

'Kylie Barton.'

Something flickered across the man's features. John wasn't positive what it was, but he pegged it as nothing good.

'She's a liar, born and bred.' The marshal picked up his pulp novel again. 'That all?'

'How do you know she's lying. You ain't looked into it yet. 'Sides, I found her collapsed on the trail. Someone beat the hell out of her.'

'Let me tell you somethin' about Miss Kylie Barton. She's lived alone too long. Always lookin' for attention from menfolk. Reckon you know the kind. She makes up stories and tries to get local folks – good folks – in trouble.'

'She didn't say it was a local man, Marshal. Fact, she couldn't even describe the fella who attacked her.'

The marshal flinched, as if he had just been caught at something, but John wasn't quite certain what. Had she been attacked by a local man before?

'Then I reckon there ain't much I can do about it anyhow, is there?'

'I take it you're not interested in looking into it?'

'Give the man a hand, folks, he's got an ounce of brains 'twixt his ears!' The marshal offered a sarcastic grin.

John fought the powerful urge to clack the man in the teeth with his Peacemaker. He could sum up the marshal in an instant. A paid-off lawdog in a rowdy town who looked the other way when need be and ignored the rest. Lazy, useless, possibly dangerous under the right circumstances. He'd seen far too many tin badges like this in his life. It sickened him.

'Maybe you won't do nothin', Marshal, but I got a mind to.' He set his Stetson on his head.

The lawdog's face took a turn toward darkness. He plainly didn't cotton to the notion of anyone investigating anything in this town.

'Just who the hell are you, stranger? What's your business here?' He tossed the pulp novel to the desk and frowned.

'Name's John Deletéreo. Reckon I'm a friend of Kylie Barton's from this point on.'

Something veiled moved across the marshal's eyes, and with it maybe a hint of concern.

'Where I heard that name before?' His tone lowered, became less challenging.

John shrugged. 'We never met.'

'I think I asked you what business you got here in this town.' The marshal stood, bracing himself against the desk with both hands.

'Reckon you did.' John smiled a thin smile, went to the door and paused with his hand on the handle. He looked back to the lawdog, whose face appeared three shades redder than when John entered.

'You know where I can find a man named Payton Galendez? Hear he has a place near these parts.'

For a moment the marshal looked about to collapse back into his chair. He might have, had his fingers not been clutching to the sides of the desk so hard they turned bone white.

'What business you got with Galendez?'

'None of yours.'

'Stay away from him. This town owes him a lot and no one will let you get close enough to hurt him.' The lawdog's gaze flicked to John's Peacemaker, then back up.

John studied the man a moment. The marshal suspected who he was, that much was plain. He knew why manhunters usually went looking for men.

'Who said I intended to?'

He left the office, the lawdog glaring after him. He had

expected Payton's Bluff to be a rowdy town but he hadn't reckoned on such antagonism. Now he knew why Kylie Barton had no interest in contacting the local law about her attack, and that just made him all the more curious about her. Perhaps it also gave him an excuse to see her again, a prospect he didn't find altogether unappealing.

CHAPTER FOUR

The Tin Dollar saloon impressed John Deletéreo as an even bigger rathole than the town of Payton's Bluff itself. As he pushed through the batwings, he paused on the landing two steps above the saloon proper, gaze roving over the room. Cowhands packed the tables, many of them too drunk to lift heads off their forearms. The tinkler-player banged away in a discordant orgy, while shouts, raucous laughter and sultry giggles from the bardoves blended into a nerve-jangling cacophony.

He noted games of chance scattered about the room, faro at one table, half-drunk players unaware of the dealer's clever sleight of hand as he pulled cards from a box emblazoned with a tiger. Bucking the Tiger they called it, but in this case the only thing getting bucked were fools from their wages.

At various other tables poker was the order of the day, along with dominoes and chuck-a-luck. One cowhand tilted sideways and vomited onto the sawdust. Another shoved him out of the chair to the floor with a guffaw, then slapped the green felt-covered table.

Across the room a fight broke out. One cowhand yelled

something about cheating that rose above the din and jumped from his chair. John expected the accuser to draw, but the man swayed, allowing time for the second fella to leap up and send a fist straight down the pike. The drunk cowhand tumbled backwards over the chair and crashed down in a cloud of sawdust, staring blankly up at the ceiling. The second man charged at him but a husky barkeep yanked a shotgun from beneath the counter and yelled a reprimand, stopping the man in his tracks. The fellow took one look at the gun, then grabbed his hat from the table and headed for the batwings. He jostled John's shoulder as he passed, paused and gave the manhunter a surly look, as if somehow blaming him for standing there. John's hand drifted beneath his open duster, settling on the butt of his Peacemaker, but the fellow lost interest and headed out into the night.

He took the two steps down to the saloon floor and threaded his way through the tables to the bar. A heavy pall of Durham smoke hung in the air. The sour stench of old booze, cow dung and sweat mixed with the reek of cheap perfume from the bargirls assailed his nostrils.

Reaching the bar, he slid out a stool and set his hat on the countertop. The bar, polished, but chipped in more places than were countable, ran along most of the north wall. One of the bardoves eyed him, raking his muscular frame with lascivious appreciation. He ignored her and from the corner of his eye he saw her drift away towards an easier mark.

'What's your poison, gent?' asked the 'keep, beefy face red, small eyes betraying boredom.

'Whiskey.' He plucked a silver dollar from his pocket and tossed it on the counter. The 'keep scooped it up, then yanked a bottle from a hutch behind him.

'Ain't seen you 'round here before, have I?' The bartender uncapped the bottle and poured the drink, then slid the glass to John.

'Just rode in.' He swallowed the whiskey in one gulp, the rotgut burning a path to his belly. It took some of the night's chill out of his bones.

'Don't get many visitors here. This town ain't the healthiest place to stop over.' The 'keep poured another drink, as the manhunter fished a second silver dollar from his pocket.

'Does seem a mite unfriendly.' He lifted the glass to his lips, this time sipping at the liquor, which tasted a hell of a lot worse the second time around.

'You could leave . . .' The barkeep grinned. 'After you finish drinkin', of course.'

John ignored the remark. 'Anyone else besides me visitin'?'

'Why you askin' questions?' The 'keep's tone came with a note of suspicion. John reckoned most folks weren't like to take kindly to strangers' curiosity in a town such as this.

'Folks get hanged for askin' questions in this town?' He put enough irritation into his tone to make the barkeep take a second look at him. In the moment their eyes locked, the beefy 'tender glimpsed something that made him back off.

'You got the look of a dead man in your eyes, fella.'

John cocked an eyebrow. 'Let's make sure that look don't jump on over to you. My meanin' clear?'

The 'keep nodded, plainly unhappy about the unsubtle threat, but unwilling to challenge it.

'You lookin' for someone? You some kind of a bounty man?'

'Might be. But I reckon that falls on the list of unhealthy propositions in this town.'

'That ain't no lie.' The bartender returned the whiskey bottle to the hutch.

'Like I asked, then, anyone else ride in tonight that you know of?' John's stare locked on the man, who shifted feet and licked his lips.

'Might be a fella.' With the statement, the 'keep's eyes drifted past John and the manhunter's head swiveled in that direction. At a table sat four men, playing poker. One of them looked half-Mex, reminding John somewhat of himself. The one sitting opposite had a passing resemblance, though lighter in complexion and brown-haired.

Two soiled doves leaned over the men, whom he took for brothers, displaying their bosoms and laughing fake laughs, feigning interest in the game.

The third player, sitting to the right of the lighter man, had the look of a ranch hand, wide in the shoulders and thick in the neck, dressed in a heavy canvas work-shirt.

The fourth fella gave him pause, dredged up some vague notion they had met somewhere, in the past. With the notion a peculiar feeling settled in his belly, one he couldn't explain. The man was little more than a boy, girlish to a degree. The smooth skin of his face was marred by fresh scratches and his long thin fingers clutched a poker-hand. His hat lay on the table in front of him.

The man's gaze suddenly lifted, as if he somehow sensed John watching him. For a instant, the man froze, and a peculiar look jumped into his eyes. His hands quivered on the cards. Gaining control of his trembling, he

47

forced his eyes back to his hand. His face washed a shade paler.

John's head turned back to the barkeep.

'Which one's new – or is it all of them?'

'One in the middle, the small guy with the pale skin. He came in about an hour ago and met up with the two Galendez boys and their ranch hand, Cleatus. The Mex-lookin' one's Jep and the other brown-haired fella's Ty.'

With the mention of the Galendez name something clutched in John's belly. 'Any relation to Payton Galendez?'

'Who the hell else would they be related to in this town? You see a sign saying Payton's Bluff on your way in?'

John nodded. 'Who's the small fella?'

'Name's Lacy. That's all I know. That's all I care to know.'

'Why's that?'

'Told you, ain't healthy to ask many questions in Payton's Bluff and that goes double for Galendez business.'

'Why don't you tell me about Payton Galendez, then.' John took another sip of his whiskey. The liquor went down hard. It tasted downright repulsive, now that he'd gotten used to it, cut with something other than water, though he couldn't tell what. Likely cow-piss from the flavor of it.

The 'keep let out a laugh.

'Hell, didn't figure there was nobody left who don't know Payton Galendez.'

'I know he's the cattle king around these parts.'

'Damn well owns the county, I figure. Ain't good to get on his bad side.'

'Reckon not.' John cast a glance behind him, back to the table. Lacy was staring at him, eyes glinting with something quickly hidden. The Galendez boys appeared more interested in their poker-hands. The cowhand tossed a silver dollar into the pile of bills and coin in the center of the table.

John's gaze returned to the 'keep.

'Where's Galendez have his spread?'

'Bit north of town. Owns damn near the entire territory.'

'He got an office here in town?'

The barman peered at John, searching for a clue as to why a stranger was so curious about Galendez.

'You know, if you're after him for some bad intent a fella could wind up lookin' at the wrong side of a casket cover for tellin' you where to find him.'

John shrugged. 'Ain't likely he'd be hard to locate, given his reputation. I got business with him, that's all.'

'From the looks of you that business usually means a rope for someone.'

'Not this time . . .' His voice dropped to nearly a whisper and the tightness in his belly cinched another notch.

'He ain't got an office in town. Doubt he'd want to associate with anyone here. Ty or Jep usually takes care of any business that needs doin' this side of the spread. Both boys come in here to blow off steam. They's more commonfolk than the old man.'

'How 'bout a woman named Kylie Barton. Know her?'

The 'keep's brow furrowed. 'Used to be the school teacher till . . . well, till she started makin' up stories.'

'What kind of stories?'

'Stories best left untold.'

'You're quite the magpie, aren't you?' John's eyes narrowed; he'd grown tired of the game now. He decided on a more direct approach. 'This story doesn't somehow go back to a Galendez, does it?'

A nervous twitch stuttered at the corner of the 'keep's left eye.

'Drink up, mister. Then move on. Best advice I can give you.' The bartender turned and walked away. John sighed and slid around on his stool, bracing his elbows against the counter. He studied the four men again, questions passing through his mind. He had come to this town seeking Payton Galendez and here were two of the cattleman's sons sitting at a table with another fellow who gave John an odd feeling of recognition for no reason he could place. The man was not a typical hardcase, but John labeled the fella as one just the same. Something about him gave off a stench, the one all human carrion put out. He'd spent too many years killing them not to detect it.

He slid from his stool, grabbed his hat, then threaded his way towards the table. If he intended to get to Payton Galendez perhaps the best way would be to confront the sons and have them take him there. He put aside any hesitation he'd felt earlier about learning the truth.

Lacy looked up as John reached the table and pulled out a chair. The other three did too, their brows furrowing and looks of surprise crossing their features.

'Who the hell invited you?' Ty Galendez asked, as John lowered himself onto the chair and set his hat onto the table.

'Now, Ty, don't go gettin' all unfriendly-like,' Lacy said, his voice effeminate and laced with a hint of sarcasm. He made a motion with one hand that sent the two bargirls on their way, both with perturbed looks. 'Mr Deletéreo here's a famous bounty man. We best show him some hospitality.' Lacy's blue eyes settled on John and again he was struck by a vague recollection of having met the man some place before.

'We met?' His gaze didn't waver from Lacy.

'Not formally . . .' Lacy smiled; it was a smile like a rattlesnake about to swallow a prairie dog. 'Thought you were dead.'

'Who's to say I ain't?' His gaze turned challenging but Lacy's eyes didn't avert.

'What do you want, Mr Deletéreo?' Jep Galendez asked, his tone less antagonistic than his brother's.

John got right to the point, shifted his attention to Jep.

'Reckon I want a meeting with your father.'

The older Galendez boy – he appeared at least five years Ty's senior – cast him a look of mixed suspicion and surprise.

'What business you got with our father?' put in Ty, who came half-way out of his seat.

John peered at the man, the hardness in his look forcing the younger Galendez back into his seat.

'Unfinished.'

'What I hear, mister bounty man, you won't get anywhere near Payton Galendez without a personal invitation.' Lacy's long fingers tightened slightly on his cards, blue veins wriggling beneath pale flesh. John noted the man's tense set, tried to size up the fellow. He saw something he didn't like, something deadly yet shallow. He couldn't tie the knot, but he would.

'Where'd you get those scratches on your face, Mr Lacy?' He asked the man direct, hoping to shake him. He saw him flinch, then recover his composure.

'Just Lacy. Don't call me mister unless . . .'

John smiled. 'Unless what, sir?'

A moment of uneasy silence dragged by. Lacy offered a sneer.

'Bravo, Mr Deletéreo. You have drawn first blood. I wouldn't recommend pushing it beyond that.' Lacy's voice turned colder, the threat clear.

John decided to test his advantage.

He reached down and drew his Peacemaker, bringing it up in a smooth blurred motion. The Galendez boys stiffened, along with the cowhand. Their eyes widened. Lacy stared, the only sign that he acknowledged the Peacemaker now aimed at his face a bobbing of his Adam's apple.

John smiled a thin smile then set the Peacemaker on the table and withdrew his hand. His eyes remained locked with Lacy's, inviting.

'You could draw on me, *Mr* Lacy, if you're of a mind. Reckon a man like you's right fast with a gun. Mine's on the table. Would take me a moment to get to it with my hands down.'

Lacy's gaze flicked to the Peacemaker, locking onto the skull carved into the ivory grip, then jumped back to John.

'I won't let you goad me, Mr Deletéreo – or should I call you Johnny Dead?'

'What the hell's the meanin' of this?' shouted Ty suddenly, crimson flooding his cheeks. 'What right you got comin' in here and treating—' He sprang from his seat, hand making a motion for the gun at his side.

Lacy uttered a sharp, 'No!' and the younger Galendez stopped in mid-motion. John's gun was already in his hand

and aimed at the man's heart.

'Sit down, Mr Galendez.' John's voice remained steady, cold. 'I won't say it twice. I got no beef with you up to this point. Let's not take it further.'

Ty Galendez hesitated and Lacy made a motion for him to sit. Jep Galendez and Cleatus sat stiff, their faces pinched and eyes filled with strained anticipation.

'Why don't you let me deal with him, Lacy?' Ty asked, plainly shaking now, but trying to cover it with bravado.

'You should thank Lacy.' John shifted his focus back to the effeminate man. 'He just saved your life.'

Ty grumbled something, face going redder, but he refrained from further movement.

'Put your gun away, Johnny.' Lacy's tone grew smug, covering a tremor. 'You won't push me into something in a bar full of innocent folk.'

'You don't strike me as a man who much cares about innocent folk.' John plucked his Peacemaker from the table and slid it into its holster. The drama had told him what he wanted to know. Lacy was deadly, but he preyed on those unable to defend themselves, those he could intimidate or back-shoot.

Lacy set his cards on the table, spread his hands.

'What is it you want here, *Johnny*?' Again something struck John as familiar; it was the way the man said his name, the inflection in his tone.

John's gaze settled on the scratches on Lacy's face.

'You didn't by chance meet up with someone on your way in tonight, did you?'

Lacy didn't miss a beat.

'Why, who might you be referring to, sir? Ah, wait, let me guess. A certain young woman?'

That confirmed his notion as to how Lacy came by the scratches and for the first time in a long spell he felt his blood heat.

'You beat her, took her money.'

Lacy laughed, a coyote sound.

'Why, I beg to differ, Mr Johnny Dead. She invited me, paid me good money to perform a service.'

'You're lying.' John said it as flat as he could manage, fighting the urge to reach across the table and throttle the little bastard.

Lacy's thin hand drifted to his shirt pocket and John tensed, ready for an instant draw. But the small man pulled out a yellow sheet of paper and tossed it on to the table before John, who glanced down at the telegraph slip.

'Read it, Mr Deletéreo.' Lacy smiled again, the expression repulsive and damned annoying.

John picked up the telegram, opened it. A bolt of heat went through his face as he read the words. He dropped the slip back to the table. Looking up, he felt at a loss for words. Lacy had caught him completely off guard and the small man knew it.

'As you can see, she brought it on herself. Did she tell you she wanted it? Wanted me to treat her rough? Begged me, in fact.' Lacy giggled a girlish sound that sent a shiver riding down John's spine.

'Reckon there's more to it than this. She don't seem the type to call on the likes of you.' Even as he said it he couldn't deny the evidence sitting right in front of him and it made something inside him freeze over.

'Tell you what, Johnny, my boy.' Lacy flipped his cards over and spread them out, showing three aces and two tens. He swept the pile of bills and coin towards him, counted off a number of them, then folded them over. Tossing them to John, he grinned. 'Tell her I am refunding her money, after all. Wouldn't be sportin' of me to take it from her since I have no intention of completing the task she hired me for. Hell, pretty woman like that . . . let's just say it was my pleasure.'

John wanted to pound the grin off the man's face, was barely able to stop himself from doing just that. He scooped up the folded bills and tucked them in a pocket. He would return them to her, but with some questions. He reckoned Lacy wasn't giving them back unless he had something bigger in mind. That would bear watching. For the moment he had his own business to attend to and a measure of disillusion with the woman he'd thought of helping had set in.

He would receive no invite from the Galendez boys tonight, however. He would have to approach the elder cattleman on his own.

Standing, he plucked his hat from the table.

'Reckon this won't be our last meeting, Lacy. Keep that in mind.' He set his hat on his head.

Lacy's grin withered and he remained quiet. John headed for the batwings, never completely taking his gaze from the table.

Lacy could barely contain the tremor threatening to shudder through him as he watched John Deletéreo depart. Now *there* was something he hadn't goddamn counted on. Ever.

What the hell did the manhunter want with the Barton woman? Had she summoned him as well? That made no sense. Deletéreo wasn't a hired killer, at least, not of Lacy's ilk. He rode on the side of the law, or, more accurately, astride it.

The blood drained from Lacy's face and he noticed the other men staring at him.

'You look like you've seen a ghost...' Jep Galendez said, face pinched.

Lacy nodded. 'Damn well might have.'

'Why didn't you let me take him on?' Ty demanded, face still reddened and muscles knotting to either side of his jaw. 'He admitted he's lookin' for my dad.'

Lacy eyed the hotheaded Galendez boy, coddling a strong dislike for him.

'You done that you'd be starin' up at the wrong side of the grave. That man's a professional killer.'

'Ain't you?' Ty's voice issued a challenge, one that hinted Lacy might be a coward. The little killer's dislike for the younger Galendez strengthened. Strong enough to put lead in him, though he reckoned he needed no real excuse for that. Fact, he enjoyed killin' too much, but right now it didn't fit with his plan to extort more money than he'd already been paid from the old man.

'You best watch your tongue, boy.' Lacy shifted his gaze to the cowhand, Cleatus, who had remained mostly quiet throughout the night. Cleatus was a reformed hardcase, of that much Jep Galendez had informed him earlier. That made the man the perfect messenger. 'You, follow that man and test him.'

Cleatus's eyes widened. The ranch hand was no fool, nor as hotheaded as the younger Galendez.

'What the hell you mean, test him? I saw how fast he was earlier. Cain't say it'd be smart takin' him on.'

Lacy's eyes narrowed.

'He's fast with a gun but men like that can't fight. Beat the hell out of him.'

'Now wait just a minute . . .' Jep started, concern jumping into his eyes. 'Ain't no need of that. You shouldn't have beat that girl, either, just scared her.'

Lacy's gaze swung to Jep, cold, like a lizard's stare.

'That man might be a danger to your father, son. I reckon we best send him a right strong message to ride on out before he takes a notion to show up on your pa's doorstep. I'm doin' him and your pa a favor.'

'He's got a point, Jep,' Ty said, too eager to agree, likely because his pride had taken a licking. 'An' that girl was gonna have me killed, after all. Who cares what happened to her?'

'Dad said he didn't want her hurt, Ty.' Jep stared down his younger brother. 'I figure I know why . . .'

Ty Galendez averted his gaze, guilt twisting on his face. He turned to Cleatus.

'Go,' he said. 'Do what Lacy tells ya.'

Cleatus looked at Jep, who reluctantly nodded.

'Reckon you best tell him to ride on out and leave Pa alone. That's it.'

Cleatus stood, looking none too happy over the assignment. He headed for the batwings, then stepped out into the night.

'We best get back to your pa,' Lacy said, finishing up his whiskey and standing.

Jep gave him a puzzled look.

'Shouldn't we wait till Cleatus gets back?'

Lacy gazed at the batwings, the thin smile back on his face.

'He ain't comin' back.'

*

Where had he seen Lacy before?

The question stuck in John Deletéreo's mind like a burr as he headed along the boardwalk towards the hotel. He had boarded his horse at the livery and slung his saddle-bags over his shoulder. Somewhere a scream singed the night. He reckoned he wanted no part of whatever it was, something he had in common with the town's law, no doubt.

A few townsfolk staggered by him, cowhands drunk and looking for a place to fall down, or else for their horse, so they could somehow find their way back to their respective ranches. But much of the activity had thinned out from earlier.

The night had grown colder, or was that simply his innards freezing over? He knew Lacy from somewhere and he knew damned well Lacy knew him, beyond the reference to that pulp novel. The notion troubled him but no more than the telegram the little turd had shown him. Kylie Barton was involved far deeper than she'd let on. At least her actions earlier made perverted sense now.

Not only had she seen the face of her assailant, she had summoned him here to kill a man in cold blood.

The notion chilled him, because it created a conflict between his impression of the woman he had briefly met and the one who had sent that note. True, he didn't know her; in fact his history with her consisted of little more than an hour and most of that she'd been unconscious. But his ability to judge folks told him that a deeper truth existed to Kylie Barton beyond the lies and the evidence in the telegram.

A sound pulled him from his reverie and he stopped, turning to look behind him.

Shadows bathed the boardwalk. He thought he caught a flash of movement, someone stepping back into the darkness of an alleyway, but he couldn't be sure. He'd barely caught the sound, the scuffing of a boot on board, yet his nerves tingled with that manhunter's sixth sense.

He was being followed.

He stepped off the boardwalk, letting himself go loose and giving the impression he was unaware of anyone trailing him. He crossed the street and sauntered toward the hotel, a block down. A scuffing sound reached his ears again, someone a few paces back, someone clumsy, likely a hair off sober.

He glanced behind him, spotted the man stepping off the boardwalk, framed by the light of a hanging lantern. Cleatus, the Galendez ranch hand. The man stopped, knowing he was caught, then suddenly charged forward.

John was in motion a split second later, duster swirling around him as he whirled and darted for an alley a half-dozen feet to his left. He tossed down his saddle-bags and the shadows swallowed him.

Cleatus lumbered into the alley, halted, a puzzled look welding to features barely visible in the bone-colored patch of moonlight. The cowhand inched forward a step, searching the darkness ahead of him for any sign of his quarry. Tensing visibly, Cleatus blew out a disgusted grunt.

'Where the hell are you, manhunter?'

John seemed to appear from the shadows. Cleatus started, fear jumping onto his face, eyes widening.

John stood there, the icy breeze jostling the folds of his duster, moonlight glinting in his brown eyes.

'Why were you followin' me?' he asked, voice flat.

'I . . . I . . .' Cleatus licked his lips. 'You best leave Payton Galendez be. Get the hell out of this town and don't look back.' The man's voice trembled; he clearly had no taste for the job and John reckoned Lacy or the boys had forced him into it.

'I'd ask if you were going to make me but that would sound horribly childish, wouldn't it?' No humor came with the words.

Cleatus remained still a moment, as if considering the wisdom of enforcing his threat. Whether stupidity or fear, something flickered in his eyes and he charged.

He threw a winging punch as John faded sideways. The punch missed and the manhunter snapped a sharp left hook into the man's jaw.

Cleatus staggered, balance suspect in the first place, the blow crisp and stunning in the second. He righted himself, whirled to see where the manhunter was standing and launched another clumsy blow.

John pivoted, brought up his leg in a side kick that connected just below the cowhand's ribs. The impact sent the man stumbling into the wall of a building. He hit hard, but spun and used the rebound to hurl himself at the manhunter again.

He was an unskilled, clumsy fighter, but game. John stepped in as the man came forward, delivering a straight-armed right that collided with the attacker's jaw with a sound of a gunshot.

Cleatus's eyes flashed blank. He shot backwards, arms flailing, blood bubbling from his mashed lips.

He hit the wall again, stood stock-still, staring at John Deletéreo, eyes reflecting a life-or-death decision at war in his mind. John knew which the cowhand would pick, but he had no desire to kill the man for doing the job he'd been forced into.

John's hand swept to his Peacemaker. The weapon came from its holster in a blur, then made a hideous clacking sound as its cylinder struck Cleatus in the temple.

Cleatus let out a bleat and his legs wobbled. He slid down into a sitting position against the wall.

John knelt before him, pressing the Peacemaker's barrel against the man's forehead.

'You go back and tell Lacy or whoever sent you I ain't one for stupid games. Next time they try a fool stunt like this they best make funeral arrangements for whoever they send.'

Cleatus nodded, eyes glazing with moisture.

John stood, holstered his Peacemaker and began to walk from the alley.

It wasn't often he misjudged a man, made a mistake, but he did now. Whether it came from blind fear or wounded pride John would never know, but he heard Cleatus rise to his feet, then the tell-tale sound of steel sliding against leather.

His heart seemed to stopped beating. He whirled, hand sweeping for the Peacemaker and bringing it level in a move that defied the eye.

A blast thundered through the chill autumn night.

Cleatus dropped the gun in his hand and peered down at the swelling blossom of scarlet on his shirt. With a gurgle blood bubbled from his lips, then he fell face first to the ground and lay still.

'You damned fool . . .' John's whispered words carried a note of disgust and anger at Lacy and the Galendez brothers for wasting a man's life. The manhunter holstered his Peacemaker, unconcerned that the sound of gunfire would attract anyone in this town. He didn't have to examine the body to know Cleatus was dead. He said a silent prayer, and shook his head.

He gathered up his saddle-bags and walked to the hotel, his soul heavy. No matter how many men he killed, no matter how many deserved it, the taking of a life always left him cold inside. Cleatus had given him no choice, but it didn't change the feeling.

He entered the hotel, a seedy-looking place holding old furniture with worn seats and a layer of dust coating the scuffed floorboards. Lanterns burned at the front desk and on various small tables about the lobby. A man with a visor looked up as John approached.

'You lookin' for a room?'

John nodded, face grim.

'Open ended.' He plucked bills from his pocket and tossed them on the counter. The clerk turned a register around and passed him a quill-pen and an ink-bottle.

The hotel man peered at the signature with indifference, then slid him a key.

'Second floor, room three. You be needin' any women?'

He shook his head. 'There's a body in the alley next door.' He would neglect to mention how it got there.

The clerk shrugged and closed the register.

'Lemme know if you change your mind on the women. I make ten percent on each.'

John inclined his head and went up the stairway against the south wall. The hallway was gloomy, one wall lantern casting a sickly glow over the torn paper on the walls and threadbare carpet.

Reaching the room, he entered, tossing his saddle-bags to the floor near the darkened shape of a bureau. He located a lantern and fished a lucifer from his pocket. After lighting the wick, he surveyed the dingy little room. A sagging mattress with a heavy wool blanket, damn near as much dirt on the floor as in the street and peeling green foiled wallpaper. A bureau with a pitcher and basin stood to the left of the door and a hardbacked chair sat in a corner. The room stank of old cigarette smoke and piss. The temperature was cold enough to see his breath.

He went to the window, gazed through the frosted pane into the night. The streets were nearly deserted now, though occasional noises from the saloon reached his ears.

He didn't know what he expected to find on riding into Payton's Bluff, other than an answer to his past, but the events that had taken place over the past few hours weren't it. A woman attacked and beaten by a man she had hired to kill another, and a hellhole town where death had little meaning. Hell of a way to end a journey.

He walked over to the bed and stripped off his duster, shirt and trousers, tossing them to the chair in the corner. As he stepped into the lantern-light, scars marring his chest and side seemed to glow with a life of their own. Flame flickered in his dark eyes.

He settled on to the bed and he pulled the blanket over himself, exhaustion filling his muscles with lead. His mind drifted, sleep coming quickly.

And again he dreamt of the day he died.

CHAPTER FIVE

The next morning found John Deletéreo riding the trail to Kylie Barton's homestead. He noted on his way out that the cowhand's body had vanished from the alley, but violent death appeared a common occurrence in Payton's Bluff; likely no one paid any mind to another corpse.

The sun came over the trees in a brassy blaze, chasing away the night mists and melting the thick coating of frost. Water dripped from boughs and bare branches, sparkling liquid diamonds. The temperature climbed enough to raise sweat on his brow. The musky scent of the rotting leaves filled his nostrils, a welcome change from the foul odors of Payton's Bluff.

Somewhere in the forest morning birds chirped and it would have been peaceful at another time, in another place. For the moment his thoughts remained tangled over the Barton woman, his own purpose for riding to Payton's Bluff, and a man named Lacy.

He'd spent a restless night trapped in nightmares of that day two years ago, the day he lost Clarissa . . . the day he died. The nightmares always left him saddled with renewed grief. He reckoned he should have moved on by now, though he had little idea to what. The man who murdered Clarissa was faceless, had vanished into the countryside. No chance of tracking him; God knew he had spent long enough trying.

Since that day John Deletéreo had fallen into the pages of legend, and it afforded him a measure of peace, though not as much as he had hoped. Perhaps if he had quit manhunting completely he could have quietly faded into the West with his grief and a bottomless whiskey bottle. But something drove him on, something nebulous and dark. He couldn't be sure what; sometimes he figured it was an irrational idea that he would someday catch up with Clarissa's murderer, though he consciously accepted that after all this time, it was damned unlikely. Other times he believed it was simply because he had nothing else left in his life. Manhunting was his sole identity – at least, it had been until two weeks ago when his mother passed, leaving him a wax-sealed envelope containing a letter that explained part of the riddle.

The part he'd come to Payton's Bluff to seek out.

Who was John Deletéreo? He'd have that answer soon enough. But would it define him beyond a man who delivered justice? A man who spent his days alone and his nights trapped in blood-drenched memories?

That question had haunted him over the past two weeks on his journey to Colorado. He knew damn well the answer might do nothing more than provide a heritage he could lay no claim to. But surely even that was better than having no roots at all.

He sighed, thoughts shifting to his encounter with Lacy at the saloon. A killer, yet at the same time a snake in the grass. Lacy had had ample opportunity to make his move face to face last night. John wasn't entirely certain he could have reached his gun in time to prevent Lacy from drilling him – if the man was as fast a draw as John expected him to be. But Lacy hadn't seized the opportunity. Instead he'd sent an innocent cowhand to his death.

That made Lacy a coward in John's estimation. A dangerous coward, because his type preyed on the weak, the defenseless, the terrified. Anyone one else he'd be inclined to back-shoot.

Despite thinking hard on it, John had been unable to define the sense of familiarity he got from the man. Yet he *had* encountered him before; of that much he felt certain.

Kylie Barton had encountered Lacy, too, on a darkened trail. Would she admit that when he confronted her today?

The woman puzzled him. Evidence told she had summoned Lacy to Colorado to murder a man. Why? John had no idea at this point, but it was a damn foolish move for a woman alone: irrational, unless some highly charged emotion lay behind it. The marshal had called her a liar, so had the barkeep; those lies had something to do with a Galendez. But were they lies or was there some deeper explanation? The marshal couldn't be trusted any more than Lacy, in John's estimation, but could he trust the word of a woman who'd already concealed facts about her attack from him?

Was she simply too frightened to reveal the truth? Ashamed? He intended to make a stab at finding out. Since it involved the Galendez family, that made it his business, he reckoned. And rationalize it as he would, it didn't cover the fact that he plain found himself wanting to see her again. Since meeting her last night he'd been unable to get her out of his mind.

He'd spent the past two years alone. Since Clarissa's death he'd never felt the desire to be with other women, not saloon girls nor women he met on cases. But Kylie Barton was different. Maybe it was the pain he glimpsed in her eyes, maybe it was something else. Maybe he was just tired of being solitary.

A twinge of guilt took him at the thought and he whispered an apology to Clarissa's memory. He hoped she'd understand.

The forest thinned, opening into the small spread nestled in a clearing a hundred yards distant. Spotting movement, his eyes narrowed. Kylie Barton stood in the small garden near the house, chopping at decaying vines with a hoe. The place appeared more ramshackle in the daylight. He reckoned she either hadn't been able to hire someone to conduct repairs or couldn't afford to.

He heeled the bay towards her. Her head came up as he approached, eyes widening. Her auburn hair was pulled back, tucked beneath a kerchief. A blouse fashioned of wagon canvas and a heavy skirt did little to accentuate her curves. Bruises showing livid on her face and her bottom lip remained puffy, but she still radiated a gentle beauty that sent a tingle down his spine. In the bright morning sunshine she looked less like Clarissa, but that didn't lessen the attraction he felt for her.

Reining up before the garden, he saw alarm flash into her eyes. Her gaze darted to a Winchester propped up against the house, then back to him. Her anxiety eased a measure when he gave her a small nod and reassuring smile.

'Mornin', ma'am.' He lifted his Stetson a fraction in greeting.

She regarded him suspiciously, fingers tightening against the hoe handle, bleaching.

'Mister . . .' Her voice trembled with an edge of nervousness. 'What brings you back here?'

He ducked his chin towards the Winchester.

'You can fetch your rifle if you like. I'll wait.'

She glanced at the rifle again, then back to him, as if weighing his offer and deciding he'd passed a test.

'I reckon that won't be necessary.'

Shifting in the saddle, he frowned.

'Saw the marshal last night. Told him 'bout your trouble here.'

Her expression dropped and she looked down at the ground for a long moment. When her head came back up her face had flushed and she offered an insincere smile.

'I reckon he told you he'd form a posse and get right on tracking down that man.'

He almost laughed.

'Not exactly. He's as useless as a lawdog gets.'

She uttered a thin chuckle, an honest expression this time.

'That's why I told you I wouldn't bother.'

'Not exactly what you said, if I recollect. You said you didn't see the man who attacked you and it would do no good.'

Her eyes narrowed, as if she were searching for the meaning behind his words.

'What are you sayin', mister?'

'Call me John.'

'You didn't answer me.' Her hands tightened further on the hoe, and her frame tensed.

John's head lifted and for a moment he gazed out at the

woods, then looked back to her. He sighed.

'Met a man at the saloon last night. Arrogant fella, goes by the name of Lacy.'

She started and her lips trembled, but she quickly brought herself under control. Her eyes darted and her body seemed to sag under the weight of her thoughts.

' 'Fraid I don't know him.'

'Funny, he seemed to know you. Fact, he said you had business with him that brought him to Payton's Bluff.'

He watched her closely, saw her begin to shake, though she struggled to prevent it. Her teeth clenched, the muscles to either side of her jaw bunching and rippling. She couldn't hold his gaze and looked out towards the woods. Her face drained a shade paler.

'I don't know what you are talkin' about. Please . . . go away now. I have work to do.' Her voice had dropped to a fragile tremolo.

He reached into a shirt-pocket beneath his duster and pulled out the folded bills Lacy had given him. He tossed them to the ground before her feet. She looked down at the bills, eyes widening a notch, but made no move to pick them up.

'Lacy asked me to refund your money.' His hands tightened on the reins and the bay nickered. 'You need me and decide to come clean you can find me at the hotel, room three. I'll help if you'll let me.'

She remained frozen to the spot, lips pressed in a tight line. He tipped his finger to his hat-brim and swung his mount around, gigging it into an easy gait towards the trail.

Kylie Barton stared at the money lying on the ground for

long moments. She wanted to pick it up, cry out her thanks to God for returning her savings, but somehow she saw the money as tainted now, blood-money, intended to buy a man's death and taken from her by a pure killer. An irrational thought, she expected: silly. That money would allow her to move on, leave this awful place and start anew somewhere else.

Alone. Still.

A tear slipped from her eye as she bent and touched the money, eventually picking it up and stuffing it into a pocket of her skirt. She straightened and gazed out in the direction of the trail, but saw no sign of the man who'd offered to help her. Why hadn't she just told him the truth? He must know some of it already since he'd met Lacy. Yet how could she risk trusting him when no one in town believed a word she said? If he had spoken with the marshal about the attack surely that no-good lawdog had called her a liar. Why would he even bother offering his help after that? Who was he really?

A man. And men couldn't be trusted. Plain and simple truth. They only took from her or left prematurely when the Lord came to call.

She heaved the hoe into the air and began hacking at the decaying squash-vines. She brought the implement down over and over, each swing harder than the previous, until sweat poured down her face and her muscles quivered with exhaustion.

A moment later she hurled the hoe, letting out an anguished scream. She dropped to her knees, tears gushing from her eyes, and sobbed uncontrollably for a very long time.

*

Marshal Tom Studdard stared at the yellow telegram slip on his desktop. Deep furrows creased his brow and dark pouches nested beneath his eyes.

It was impossible. Dead men just didn't rise up and walk away. They didn't ride into Payton's Bluff, either.

A few moments after John Deletéreo left his office last night Marshal Studdard had stepped over to the telegraph office and made Schneider send a post off to a friend working for the Pinkertons. A messenger had returned with the answer a few moments ago.

It told him a dead man had ridden into his town.

A chill skittered down his back at the thought. He knew the name was damned familiar to him the moment he heard it. John Deletéreo, the deadliest bounty man this side of the Mississippi. What the hell business did such a man have with Galendez?

Christ on a crutch, things were starting to fall apart. He'd known it was a damned likely probability the moment he learned Sutter had given that Barton gal Lacy's name, only to be confirmed when Schneider blabbed about the telegram she'd sent. He'd learned about it too late to stop the message from going, but in time to warm Galendez and make contingency plans. Galendez was a man of means, so a second telegram had gone out, offering three times the money to Lacy to scrub the job and put the fear of God into the Barton woman. But something had gone wrong, the way Studdard had known it would. Things had gotten too damned complicated and too many variables existed, too many chances for unpluggable leaks to spring up.

Chance had also played a bastard role. A manhunter had ridden in and discovered the woman hurt and spouting a story about an attack.

How much had she told Deletéreo? Not enough, obviously, or that manhunter would have been raising holy hell by now. She was likely too scared; at least that part of Galendez's plan had held up. But for how long? She might break after last month's incident and scandal. Woman like that had some God-driven cause to tell the truth instead of just pushing it aside, way a man would. They might have to do something about her eventually, despite what Galendez said. More was at stake here than just the family's reputation. Ty Galendez paid Studdard good money to make sure things ran smoothly and no one looked too deeply at anything associated with Galendez business. If the old man ever discovered some of the deals Ty pulled, how he came by cattle so cheap, brand expertly altered, there'd be hell to pay and the cash-cow would be slaughtered.

He gave in to a case of the shakes. First order of business was the manhunter, though. He was the most dangerous. Kylie Barton might open her mouth, but Deletéreo would open fire.

But how the hell did you deal with a dead man?

The door rattled open and Studdard jolted, letting out a burst of air. Damn, but his nerves were strung tighter than an overtuned fiddle-string.

They got even tighter the moment his gaze met the man in the doorway.

Lacy stepped into the office and closed the door behind him.

'Afternoon, Studdard.' A smug expression hung on the little killer's face. The man gave Studdard the willies, though they were associates of a sort, having worked together a couple times in the old days. Studdard recollected just how vicious Lacy could be, how he liked to torture weaker folks, like pulling the wings off a butterfly before driving a nail through its back. Lacy was a predator of the worst sort, maybe even worse than that manhunter fellow. At least the manhunter had compunction, a trait Studdard little admired except when it meant saving his own hide.

'We have a problem, Lacy.' Studdard's voice shook. He indicated the telegram on his desk.

Lacy stepped over to the desk, picked up the slip and scanned the words, then tossed it back down.

'I'm aware of it. He came into the saloon last night.'

Studdard's eyes widened.

'Why the hell didn't you kill him then? In this town no one would have said a word.'

Lacy averted his eyes, went over to the window and gazed out into the afternoon street. Folks shuffled about, a bit more reserved in the daylight.

'Well?' Studdard asked, sensing some sort of hesitancy in the boyish killer.

'Figured I'd feel him out first.' Was Lacy lying? Studdard had a notion he was, but also had the good sense not to challenge the point. 'Sent Cleatus after him to do that job.'

'Cleatus's body was found in the alley next to the hotel this morning. We dumped it out in the woods for the buzzards.'

Lacy nodded. 'Figured as much when he didn't come back last night. Just came here to have it confirmed.'

'John Deletéreo's a right dangerous man, Lacy. We got to do something about him.'

'You want to take him on?' Lacy turned to Studdard,

drilling him with his soulless gaze.

The marshal shuddered, half from that gaze and half from the thought of going up against the manhunter.

'No, but you could.'

Lacy worked his jaw back and forth, but didn't reply. Studdard wondered about that but didn't spend much time thinking on it.

The marshal picked up the telegram and waved it.

'John Deletéreo died two years ago, Lacy. Did you know that? We got a dead man ridin' into town and taking up with that Barton woman.'

'I know.'

Studdard's brow scrunched in surprise.

'How do you know? I only just got the telegram myself.'

'I saw his grave.' A peculiar look came over Lacy's face, one Studdard couldn't read. The boyish killer turned back to the window.

Studdard shook his head.

'Damn strange, if you ask me. The man I talked to last night wasn't no spook, that's for damn sure. No spook killed Cleatus, neither.'

Lacy smiled. 'Yet the fact remains . . . John Deletéreo, manhunter, perished in an ambush two years ago along with his woman. Their graves sit on a hilltop in New Mex.'

Studdard shuddered again, wishing Lacy hadn't said it with such conviction. It was impossible, simply impossible. He'd thought it a hundred times since receiving the telegram and he still thought it.

'We got to do something about him. Kill him.'

Lacy's gaze settled on the marshal again, who tossed the telegram back onto the desk and sank further into his chair.

'You just don't kill a man like Johnny Dead so easy, Studdard. That telegram ought to tell you that. You have to plan it out.'

'How do you propose to do that?'

'The fella who told that Barton woman how to contact me, told her what I am.'

'Sutter? What good's he? He's just a drunk now, though I reckon he's got a memory like a steel trap 'bout the days we used to ride together. He's also got no loyalties. If not for him tellin' Galendez about you Ty would likely be dead by now.'

'Where can I find him?'

'Only two places he'd be, either at his shack down at the edge of Custer Street or at the saloon with a whore, squan-derin' his new-found bank account. Don't see what good it will do to talk to him, though.'

Lacy laughed a cold laugh. 'Don't intend talkin' to him. He's gonna help me with a contingency plan.'

Studdard's brow bunched tighter and he had half a mind to question Lacy about that further, but knew better.

'What about the Barton gal?'

'She didn't tell Deletéreo anything. Fact, he was damn surprised when I showed him why she brought me here. Don't reckon she'll be a problem, but I can always throw another scare into her till the old man comes to his senses and just lets me shut her mouth permanently.'

'Why don't you just kill her anyway?'

Lacy raised an eyebrow.

'And spoil my nice soft job being Ty's bodyguard? Galendez has a lot of money, Studdard. I aim to acquire a goodly share of it.'

'You always were a bastard, Lacy.' It just slipped out and

Studdard instantly regretted it when Lacy's expression darkened.

'You're mighty lucky we used to ride as pards, Studdard.'

With that Lacy went to the door and stepped out into the afternoon sunlight.

John rode into town two hours past noon, having spent most of the time trying to get his thoughts in order but finding little success with the effort. He'd discovered a stream and sat fishing with a makeshift branch-pole, catching nothing but a sore tailbone.

Payton's Bluff still stank and daylight did nothing to pretty it up, though it appeared more sedate. He kept his horse to a slow walk, gaze sweeping over the folks wandering along the boardwalks. A couple men slouched against walls of buildings, still sleeping off the previous night's revelry. Some folks gave the men kicks on their way by, laughing. A damned peculiar form of entertainment, in his estimation.

He sighed. The sooner he finished his business here the better. He doubted Kylie Barton would provide him with a reason to stick around, after his talk with her this morning. She didn't trust him enough to tell him any more than he already knew; he didn't see anything he could do to change that. She was too frightened. In her eyes he had seen pain, maybe even hopelessness, but he couldn't force her to accept his help. He'd offered. Now the choice was hers.

He reckoned he'd keep an eye on Lacy just the same, in case he made some move on the Barton woman and until he figured out just where they'd met before. He would have preferred slapping the boyish hardcase in a cell but Kylie wouldn't press charges and John couldn't prove Lacy had set up Cleatus to try killing him. He reckoned Lacy had a Wanted dodger on him somewhere, but in this town he'd be unlikely to get the marshal to help him locate one. At some point he'd ride for the county marshal and see what he could dig up, but first he'd follow through with his own reason for coming to Payton's Bluff.

The door to the marshal's office opened, dragging John from his thoughts. He watched Lacy step out onto the boardwalk. The sight solidified his suspicions of the lawdog's uselessness.

Lacy's gaze roved, halting as it came to rest on John. The killer strode to a post and leaned against it, fishing a silver case from his pocket. He withdrew a cigarette, poked it between his lips, then returned the case to his pocket. He lit up, tossed the match to the ground and blew smoke into the air, keeping his eyes on John the entire time.

John reined up, looking down, a measure of irritation crawling through his nerves at the sight of the little killer.

'You got a hell of a yellow streak, Lacy.'

Lacy raised an eyebrow, a spark of anger in his eyes.

'I'm afraid I don't know what you're talking about, Johnny boy.'

'You sent Cleatus after me last night, knowing that man couldn't hope to best me.'

Lacy cocked his head. 'Did I? Don't recall. Cleatus was kind of drunk and just staggered out after you, from what I could see. Reckon he took offense to you disgracin' his employer's son way you did. Hell of a man, that Cleatus. Valiant, don't you think?'

John stared at the man, seeing an utter lack of emotion

and compassion. Lacy didn't care who died to meet his ends. The cold blue eyes said it all; here was a man with no morals, no decency, no soul.

John leaned forward, forearms resting against the horn.

'You listen to me, Lacy. The moment you cross another line I'll be there waiting. Don't give a damn whether the law here protects you or not.'

Lacy laughed but the expression held a hint of nervousness.

'Ah, so dramatic, sir. You really should try the stage.' The little killer paused, took a drag from his cigarette. 'Since we're laying our cards on the table, reckon I could say the same for you, Johnny boy. This is Galendez territory. Town has its own law and its own rules.' Lacy threw down his cigarette and stepped off the boardwalk, face going dark. 'Stay out of my way, manhunter. Or this time you'll truly be Johnny Dead.' Lacy walked off towards the saloon and John watched him go. He'd let anger get the better of him, though he knew Lacy wouldn't be goaded into anything up front. Still, it satisfied him that he had gotten under the man's skin. He hoped that wouldn't come back to haunt him.

The door burst open and Lacy stood there framed in the anemic light that came through a window in the seedy room, gun in hand. The room was little larger than an outhouse and was located on the floor above the saloon. It was one of five chambers where whores took marks to do their business.

On the bed, a blonde jerked the covers up over her bare breasts and let out a startled chirp. Standing beside the bed, a man in a unionsuit froze, gaze riveting to Lacy.

Stubble peppered the man's lined face and his eyes were bloodshot to such an extent that their true color was no longer discernible.

'Lacy . . .' the man muttered. 'W-What you want?'

The little killer in the doorway smiled the snake smile.

'Good, you know me.'

The man blinked. 'Saw your face on a poster. Kept up with your travels. You're sort of a hero of mine.' The man had more fear than pride in his voice. Lacy enjoyed that. Sutter was terrified and that made murder all the more delicious.

Lacy waved the gun towards the bed, aiming at the girl.

'*You* . . . get out.'

A panicked look washed across the blonde's make-up-caked features.

'But I ain't got no clothes on—'

'I said *get out*.' Lacy's voice lowered, deadly in tone. He drew back the hammer on his Smith & Wesson.

The girl, casting modesty aside, leaped from the bed and ran past him, naked. A few moments later, he heard a chorus of cheers arise from below and knew she had reached the saloon proper.

Lacy stepped into the room and closed the door. Sutter shifted feet and began to go for the trousers hanging over the edge of the bed.

Lacy stopped him with a motion of the gun. 'You won't be needin' 'em.'

Sutter started shaking. 'But I done you a favor by getting Galendez to pay you more. I sent you work.'

Lacy's smile widened. 'I appreciate that, I truly do. Now you're going to do me another favor, friend.'

Sutter relaxed a measure. 'Sure thing, Mr Lacy.

Anything. Anything you want.'

Lacy's face darkened. 'I hate being called mister.'

Sutter opened his mouth to apologize, but never got the first word out.

Lacy pulled the trigger. The blast thundered through the small room, pounding against his eardrums.

Sutter jumped backwards, a starburst of crimson exploding across the front of his unionsuit. He made fish movements with his mouth, gazed down at the blood bubbling from his chest.

He started to slide down the wall, then suddenly pitched forward and hit the floor face first.

'Thanks for all your help . . .' whispered Lacy, holstering his gun and going to the body.

CHAPTER SIX

At sunrise the next day, John Deletéreo stopped at a café and downed a quick breakfast of beefsteak, warm biscuits and steaming Arbuckle's. After another fitful night plagued by ghosts from his past that tangled with images of the present, it took nearly the entire pot to drive the exhaustion from his hide.

Lacy and Kylie Barton, the marshal and the Galendez boys. Parts of a whole or merely linked by coincidence and misfortune? He wondered. He'd ridden to Payton's Bluff for one thing and one thing alone: to discover who he was, where he came from. What happened beyond that he reckoned was of little concern. Now he wasn't so sure. The more he thought about Lacy, the more the man got under his skin and set off alarms in his mind. The more he felt sure the little bastard posed an obstacle to his business with Galendez and a danger to Kylie Barton.

The young woman also got under his skin, though in a different way. He discovered his thoughts turning to her more often than not. He wanted to know more about her, and what made her so bitter she'd hire a man like Lacy to kill a Galendez.

Maybe loneliness had caught up with him. Maybe he just missed Clarissa too much. He'd gone a spell without dwelling on the grief burned into his soul by the events of two years past. But something had opened a door to that time: those feelings and a growing doubt told him it wasn't entirely Kylie Barton. The nightmares had increased, become more acute. Agitation made his nerves dance. He wished he could narrow down exactly what elicited the feelings, but each time he thought he had a handle on something it drifted out of reach. One thing was certain: it had started the night he rode into Payton's Bluff.

Shaking from his thoughts, he downed the rest of his coffee, then stood, setting his hat atop his head. After tossing greenbacks on the table he stepped outside into the crisp morning air. The sun exploded over the horizon in a gory display of red, amber and orange. Bloody light glinted from shop windows. He noted a man doubled over a rail heaving his innards; another cowboy farther down the boardwalk staggered, bumping into posts and cursing at the non-existent dogs he stumbled over.

He went to his bay and untethered the reins. He mounted, reined around and heeled his horse into a fast gait through the rutted wide street. Locating Payton Galendez's spread would prove little problem, he reckoned. He had a general idea from the barkeep and doubted a man of such means as Galendez would spare any expense in erecting his kingdom.

A mile out the sight of the Galendez mansion confirmed that notion.

The trail melted away into rolling fields of autumn grass, valleys and low hills as far as the eye could see. In the distance, mountain peaks appeared dipped in blood, their snowy caps bathed in scarlet sunlight. A rolling mist vanished before his eyes, and frost turned to dew.

Outbuildings, arranged in an uneven horseshoe pattern, fringed the main dwelling's inner circle. Smoke billowed from a cookhouse, redolent with the scents of bacon and seared beef. He saw work-sheds, an ice-house and a spring-house – a small wooden structure built over a spring used as a cooling area for butter and milk – as well as a smoke-house, sprawling barn and a carriage-house. A bunkhouse and various other buildings, along with corrals, completed the compound. No question about it, Payton Galendez was a man of means.

Then why did your mother die so poor?

Blood heating at the thought, he choked back a measure of disgust mixed with anger. Balls of muscle at either side of his jaw rippled with tension. Some men spent their lives acquiring everything a body could want – fancy house, gold, power over an industry – while others wallowed in poverty and struggled just to stay alive. He hadn't give it much thought before, but the sight of such prosperity unearthed a burning resentment.

No, your ma was a proud woman. She wouldn't have accepted his help. You know better.

He took a deep breath, sighing, knowing that his increasing agitation was distorting his perspective. While he had expected some anger towards the man he'd never met, its intensity caught him by surprise. He hadn't counted on other factors, Lacy and Kylie Barton, augmenting what might prove an emotionally charged reaction upon eventually meeting Galendez.

Slowing his horse to an easy walk, he scanned the grounds for any sign of life. He spotted a few cattle on his way in, noting their Circle G brands. Rumor had it Galendez was well on his way to being as big as Chisum, New Mexico's cattle king. He'd amassed his fortune and herds on the blood, sweat and tears of others. For a brief spell, rumor also speculated that Galendez somehow played a game with cheap beef of questionable brands to send his empire leap-frogging above the other spreads vying for supremacy, crushing many. The rumor had been hastily squelched before it blew up into solid fact. Suspected pay-offs to the Cattleman's Association and high-placed officials saved the elder Galendez a passel of grief, the kind that often resulted in a necktie party.

John wagered that more lay behind that rumor than simply jealous competitors. Otherwise why would a man of Galendez's stature associate with a man like Lacy, a hired killer? True, plenty of ranchers hired range detectives who were little more than glorified killers, but Lacy belonged in another league.

Where did Galendez's son, Ty, come into the equation? Kylie despised the fella enough to want him dead and hire a professional assassin to that end. Someone had obviously tipped off Galendez, allowing him to circumvent the plan, likely by throwing a barrelful of money at Lacy. Yet Lacy remained in Payton's Bluff. Why? To fend off any possible future attempts by the Barton woman? John doubted that was the case. She was too scared to try such a foolish move again; Lacy had seen to that. Lacy wasn't the type to play bodyguard to a hotheaded cattleman's son, either, if John had him figured right. That meant the killer had a deeper motive, one that likely involved money, lots of it. Galendez was a rich man. Lacy planned to shake him down some-how, perhaps by threat, perhaps by ruse. Didn't matter which. A man like Lacy worked to his own ends, no one else's.

The sound of hoofbeats pulled him from his thoughts and he glanced left, beyond a corral. Two men rode hell-bent straight for him. He reined up, unbuttoning his duster to let the flaps hang at his sides, allowing him instant access to his Peacemaker should the need arise.

The riders slowed up as they approached and he got a good look at their faces. Jep and Ty Galendez. The men reined up to either side of John, both jerking Winchesters from saddle boots and swinging the muzzles towards his chest.

'Thought we made it clear you weren't welcome on Galendez land?' Ty's gaze drilled John. The younger man's eyes carried a certain cruelty that told John the boy wasn't bravado; he was three-parts temper and one-part idiot.

'I got business with your father. I aim to see him.' He said it calmly, made no sudden moves. Ty's finger was itchy on the trigger and a nervous man made mistakes.

'I could just shoot you for trespassing on Galendez land, mister.' Ty appeared eager to do just that. John held his gaze, eyes narrowing slightly.

'Wouldn't recommend you try, son.' His voice held more frost than the morning grass.

'Don't do anything stupid, Ty.' Jep Galendez eyed his younger brother with a reprimanding glare. 'You of all people know what that leads to.' Something unsaid underlied Jep's words to his brother. The younger Galendez gave his brother a sour look but relaxed his finger on the trigger.

John surveyed Jep Galendez, struck again by the resemblance to himself. The angular set of jaw, the dark eyes and mixed complexion, the build; all hinted at a common parentage. It made him more certain his mother's letter held the truth.

He noted something else in the older Galendez boy's eyes, a compassion absent in Ty's, a rationality as well.

'State your business with my father, sir.' Jep held his rifle ready, but somehow less threatening than Ty's.

John weighed his options. He might come out of a sudden draw with one Galendez dead, but the other would surely put lead in him. Still, he had little desire to tell them his true reasons for coming.

'I got news for your father. He'll want to hear it.'

Jep eyed him, searching for something, a flicker of what – recognition? in his eyes. He saw the resemblance and something about it disturbed him.

'What kind of news?' Jep asked.

'Reckon that'll be up to your father to tell you after I'm gone.'

'What the hell you botherin' with this fella for, Jep?' Ty's voice climbed in pitch. His face turned a shade redder. 'Give him to the marshal for trespassing on our land.'

'Shut up, Ty.' Jep Galendez flashed his brother a look. Ty spat in protest, then clamped his lips together in a tight grimace.

'What assurance I got you ain't here to cause him harm?' Jep shifted his attention back to John. 'I'm told you're a killer.'

'Lacy tell you that?' John cocked an eyebrow. 'Consider your source, Jep. You want to put your trust in a man like that?'

'What makes you any better?' Jep's question was delivered with honesty, not challenge.

'I hunt men who deserve it. Killers, robbers, rapists. They've been judged guilty of their crimes and pay for them.'

From the corner of his eye John saw Ty squirm in the saddle, an uneasy look turning his features. He wondered if it had any connection to Kylie Barton.

'I'll bring you in, but you'll leave your gun at the door with me. You'll be watched closely.' Jep's tone brooked no argument. It was plain the conditions were the only ones under which John would gain an audience with Payton Galendez.

He nodded. 'Reckon I can't ask for more than that.'

Jep ducked his chin towards the house. John heeled his horse into motion, the two Galendez boys riding flank.

The house was hacienda-style, sprawling and huge, with hewn roof beams that extended over the edge and a veranda that ran the length of the front. Deep-set windows and meticulously trimmed hedges ornamented the structure. Smoke curled from two chimneys. The door looked thick enough to guard a fortress.

He reined to a halt before the front steps and hopped down from his mount, the two brothers following suit, keeping their Winchesters steady on him. Ty's face welded with a sour expression that didn't change the entire time, while Jep's features stayed more complacent, yet distrustful.

Jep suddenly plucked the Peacemaker from John's holster; the manhunter made no move to stop him. They urged him up the steps and across the porch. Ty opened the door and gestured forcefully with his rifle. John stepped inside into a vestibule that led to a long hall with arched doorways to either side. The adobe was fresh-painted and exquisite colonial portraits adorned the walls on either side. The brothers guided him down the hallway to the first archway and with a nudge of the Winchesters indicated for him to enter the room.

The chamber was a drawing-room, richly furnished with Victorian furniture of dark woods, plush blood-velvet and carved legs with ball-and-claw feet. Velvet drapes of deep indigo hung to either side of large windows, through which streamed golden beams of light now that the sun had risen higher. A gild-edged harpsichord with ivory trimmings stood in a corner. Paintings of nude women by classical artists hung on the walls and a rich carpet covered the floor. A mahogany bar took up the north portion of the room, crystal decanters sitting atop its polished counter. A silver cigar box with intricate molding rested near crystal glasses.

Payton Galendez himself appeared incongruous in his surroundings, a man of affected presence. The cattle magnate turned from the window as they entered, the expression on his face shifting from placid to one of mixed annoyance and curiosity. His rich, dark hair was graying at the mutton chop side-whiskers and bushy mustache. Deep-brown eyes glittered with hard light. A burly frame told of a powerful man; his angular face and darker skin bore a passing resemblance to John. His morning-jacket was of blue silk, emblazoned with gold. Sharply creased trousers and fine leather shoes advertised his wealth.

Galendez withdrew a thin cigar from his mouth and blew out a cloud of smoke.

His hard eyes settled on his sons.

'You know I don't allow visitors during my morning smoke.' His voice held an annoyed edge. He raised an eyebrow as his focus suddenly shifted to John. A look came into his eyes, a look that said something from the past had come back to confront him. Recognition, surprise, then reined-in anger.

'Leave us alone,' Galendez said to his sons.

Jep shook his head. 'Can't, Pa. This man's a bounty man. Wouldn't be safe.'

'I know damn well who he is. This is the fella Lacy told me about. You stay, Jep. Ty, get out.'

'The hell I will—' Ty started but Payton cast him a no-nonsense look and the boy's mouth clamped shut. The younger son flashed John an angry glare, then turned on a boot-toe and left the room, muttering a curse.

Jep backed to the wall and leaned his back against it, keeping the Winchester in ready.

'Come in, Mr Deletéreo.' Payton moved over to the bar and stumped out his cigar in a silver tray. 'Drink?'

John shook his head. 'Too early in the morning.'

The man let out an abrasive laugh.

'Never too early. Well, state your business, Mr Deletéreo. You're a manhunter, work for some cattleman's organizations, I reckon. I got all the men I need, though, so if you're here for a job you're out of luck.' The bluster in his tone failed to hide the fact that he knew John hadn't come for employment.

'That include Lacy?'

'What business is that of yours?' Payton cocked an eyebrow, then selected a decanter and poured amber liquor into a wide-mouthed glass.

'The man's a killer. He can't be trusted.' John stated it matter of factly, not expecting much of a reaction from Galendez. Sizing up the man, he saw a pompous ruler without much compunction regarding whom he associated with, as long as they followed his direction and achieved his ends.

Payton Galendez swallowed a gulp of his drink and shrugged.

'So that makes him different from you how?'

A prickle of irritation at the comparison went through his nerves. The more the man spoke, the less John liked him. He saw where Ty got his manner.

'Reckon you know the difference.'

Payton gave a dismissing wave of his hand.

'Someone threatened one of my sons. I hired Lacy to see to it that that threat wasn't carried out. Nothing more to it. He's the best man for the job.'

John locked gazes with the elder Galendez. He saw no give in the man's demeanor. The cattleman was used to debate and used to getting his way in the end.

'What type of threat might that be, Mr Galendez?'

'Don't see how that's your concern.' Payton's tone became gruff. He swirled the liquor about in his glass.

'Your son worried because he's guilty of something?'

A hint of crimson invaded Payton Galendez's cheeks.

'If that's all you came here to discuss, Mr Deletéreo, I suggest you leave now and save us both the waste of time. I'm not about to disclose Galendez business to a stranger.'

'No?' John's heart stepped up a notch. 'Would it make a difference if it were a Galendez by birth?'

Jep started at the question, eyes shifting back and forth between John and his father. The elder Galendez slid on a poker face, but the rigid set of his burly frame betrayed his annoyance with the question.

'What the hell do you want here, Deletéreo? You've got five seconds to state your business before I have you hauled out on your back.'

'You recollect a woman named Emma Blake?'

The elder Galendez's eyes widened a hair. He turned away from John, stared at his glass a moment then downed the rest of the liquor in one gulp. When he turned back to the manhunter he again had control of his emotions.

'Can't say I do. Should I know this woman?'

John took a step forward, brow creasing beneath his Stetson.

'Let me refresh your memory. She married a man named Jason Deletéreo, two years *after* I was born. Gave me his name, though it rightly didn't belong to me. That man turned out to be a drunk. One day he wandered off and never came back. Don't know what the hell happened to him. But he wasn't the only one who saw fit to ride out on Emma Blake, was he, Mr Galendez?'

The cattleman shook his head, too fast.

'I'm certain I don't know what you're talking about, Mr Deletéreo. Why should this information be of concern to me?'

'Reckon it isn't. Reckon it never was. What would a rich man like you care about a woman left to fend for herself alone? A woman with child.'

'Get to the point, sir. I have a busy schedule.' The elder Galendez's voice cracked, just slightly, but enough for John to know he had gotten to him.

'I'm gettin' there, Mr Galendez. Took me twenty-five years to come by the information. Reckon the least you can do is give me a few more minutes of your time.'

The cattleman's face grew redder.

'I owe you nothing.' His voice lowered, and his gaze avoided Jep's, whose own attention was centered on his father. The older Galendez boy's hands were white from clenching the rifle too tightly.

'No, reckon you don't.' John let a thin smile filter onto his lips, but disgust boiled in his gut. 'See, Mr Galendez, Emma Blake never had the life you have. She struggled every day to raise me and provide, sometimes doing things that made her heave her belly late at night when she thought I was asleep. But I wasn't. I saw what her life did to her. I saw how it ate away her innards and made her into a bitter woman. But she was never bitter or ashamed of me, no matter that I was a bastard and everyone knew it. She made sure I had something to eat every day and made sure I got schoolin'. When I was old enough to set out on my own, I sent her money from my jobs, took care of her. Was only right after all she sacrificed for me.'

'Touching, I'm sure, Mr Deletéreo. Have you come for money for her? That what you want here?'

'No, Mr Galendez, I didn't come for money. I want nothing from you you ain't prepared to give out of the kindness of your heart, something money can't buy. I came for a piece of who I am, an answer to my past.'

'You're not making sense, sir.' The irritation in the cattleman's tone grew stronger, but a hint of guilt came through as well.

'I wouldn't expect a man like you to understand. I wouldn't expect a fella who rode off on a woman with child to care about what he left behind.'

'If you're implying I—'

'I'm implying nothing, Mr Galendez. Reckon I've gotten what I came for.' John swallowed hard. 'It's not the comfort I thought it would be.'

'Best you leave now, Mr Deletéreo. I got ranch business to attend to.' Payton's eyes turned harder and his voice dismissive. Jep's face held something akin to compassion mixed with shock.

John nodded, lips pressed into a grim line. He turned and began walking from the room.

'Mr Deletéreo . . .' the elder Galendez said behind him.

John glanced back over his shoulder, remaining silent. Galendez's face had softened a notch.

'This Emma Blake . . . is she . . . all right now?'

A trace of a smile touched John's lips.

'She's at peace, Mr Galendez. She passed away from the consumption a bit over two weeks ago. She'd had it for quite a spell. Her suffering's over.'

Payton Galendez swallowed and turned away, gazing out through the window. John headed out of the room, Jep following. When they stepped out onto the veranda, Jep handed John his Peacemaker. The manhunter slid the gun into its holster. Ty watched from the corner of the veranda, arms crossed, an angry look darkening his features.

'What you said to my father . . .' Jep said, watching John mount his bay after untethering the reins. 'That true?'

'Every word of it, God's honest. Reckon you're smart enough to put together the rest.'

Jep nodded. 'You didn't come for money? A rich man like my father attracts . . . well, you know what I mean.'

John shook his head. 'I got enough money saved. I don't want nothing from your father. Just wanted to find out who I am.'

'Reckon that makes you my . . .' Jep looked at the ground, unable to finish the sentence, then up again.

'Reckon it does.' John reined around and heeled his horse into a gallop towards the edge of Galendez land. His hands tightened on the reins and he drew a stuttering breath, fighting a wave of emotion choking his throat and shaking his being. He'd gotten what he came for true enough, but somewhere inside he had hoped it would be more. Some mysteries were best left unsolved. Maybe the past, who a man was, wasn't so much his breeding. Maybe it was more what he made of himself. In this case it would have to be.

Payton Galendez watched the manhunter ride for the edge of his property. Christ, last thing he needed was one of his mistakes showing up out of the blue. Bad enough that the Barton woman had taken a fool notion to hire a goddamned killer to go after his son. He should have realized the woman had too much spunk. She'd stood up to damn near a whole town and accused Ty of misdeed, despite the town being in Galendez's pocket. He might have admired her for that under different circumstances, but he simply couldn't let her ruin his reputation and risk the business. Bad enough Ty had done that on his own, and was still doing it, though he thought his addled pa didn't know what was going on. Did he really think his father was that stupid? Payton Galendez hadn't built an empire by shutting his eyes. He knew damn well what Ty was up to and as long as the boy didn't get caught he'd let him keep at it. Business was business, after all, no matter how one acquired it.

Crazy sonofabitch boy. He was too much like his old

man, that was the problem. He made the same mistakes, couldn't keep his hands off the women. But one thing his son didn't have from his father – the ability to clean up the messes he made.

Payton Galendez had ridden away from his problems years ago, paid off his son's when necessary. Ty would likely get his fool hide killed one of these days. The boy had no head on his shoulders when it came to self-preservation.

And Jep . . . Jep was too damned honest for his own good, for the *family's* own good. Where the hell had he gone wrong with that one?

A sound brought him from his thoughts. He turned to see Lacy standing in the entry, leaning against the jamb, smoking a cigarette. The little killer's face had a peculiar look and Galendez wondered just how long he'd been lurking beyond the doorway. Had he overheard any of the conversation with Deletéreo? Payton's face colored.

'What the hell are you doing in here so early?'

'I'm a light sleeper, Galendez. I see we had company.'

'You use the word *we* a bit too loosely. I don't like it. This is my home. You are a guest here.' Payton's tone grew harder. He was getting damned sick of that little bastard. It had been a mistake hiring him.

'I ain't concerned with what you like, Payton. I'm only concerned with doing my job.'

'Seems you got a false impression of just what that job entails. I told you not to hurt the Barton woman, just scare her. Jep tells me you beat on her.'

Lacy's cold eyes glittered, their expression unreadable.

'Wasn't my fault. She damn near scratched my face off. She's a danger. Just like that manhunter. They should both be taken care of.'

Payton's eyes narrowed. 'If by "taken care of" you mean killing—'

'Dead men don't talk. They don't pose a threat, either.'

'I told you no killing and I meant it. I won't stand for you not following my orders. Fact is, I don't have much use for you anymore, Lacy. I'll give you enough money to buy your resignation.'

'You already gave me money.' Lacy's expression turned icy. 'And you'll keep giving me money, 'less you want those rumors of brand altering to become truth in some court of law. See, like I told you, the marshal knows your son's still up to no good. He thinks you don't know, but that ain't the truth, is it?'

Payton shifted feet, letting out a heavy sigh.

'What the hell do you really want, Lacy?'

Lacy giggled, a girlish sound that set Galendez's nerves further on edge.

'You know what I want. More money, a never-ending stream of it. I've grown comfortable here, Payton my boy. I like not having to work for my wages. I like having access to whatever I want when I want it. Gotta admit, it's better than roaming around waitin' for jobs that don't pay enough. Now I can sit pretty and enjoy the good life, just like you.'

'Please . . . leave the Barton woman alone.'

'Do I detect a hint of guilt in your voice, Payton my man?' Lacy took a drag on his cigarette, blew out the smoke. 'Ah, yes, I believe I do. It's one thing to protect your son, but ruining a decent woman's reputation, making her out a liar, that bothered you in some way, didn't it? You got a shred of honor. That's a disgusting weakness, Galendez. Surprises me outa you. Best get rid of it.'

Lacy pushed away from the jamb and turned to walk out of the room, pausing. Payton Galendez fumed so much inside that words stuck in his throat. He wished he had the guts to shoot Lacy in the back.

Lacy turned back to Galendez.

'In case you got any ideas 'bout siccin' that manhunter on me, Payton, I left a letter in the hands of our good friend, the marshal. He's got it tucked away nice and safe somewhere with instructions to go straight to the newspapers with evidence of your son's, shall we say, *indiscretions* with cattle buying should anything happen to me.' His eyes glittered with superiority. He knew he had the old man by the balls and that was a position Payton Galendez wasn't used to and little cared for. It told him just how the Barton woman felt.

Jep Galendez stepped from the veranda and walked a few paces out into the trimmed yard. He watched John Deletéreo ride away, a heaviness settling over his conscience. He believed what the manhunter had said, had somehow suspected as much even before the discussion with his father. He had seen it in the manhunter's face, his features. They looked so much alike, him and Deletéreo, enough to be brothers. Now he knew why.

'Christ, Jep, why'd you make a fool outa me in front of that manhunter?' Jep turned to see Ty coming up behind him, a bee in his bonnet, as usual. He was getting damned sick of his brother's rants. When was that sonofabitch going to grow up and stop risking the Galendez name?

'I didn't have nothin' to do with it. You made a fool out of yourself just fine.'

'The hell I did! You know that manhunter has it in for us all.'

'Does he?' Folding his arms, Jep eyed his brother with a harsh look. 'I reckon he doesn't. I reckon he's just a man lookin' for his roots and now that he's found them he wishes he hadn't.'

A puzzled expression came onto Ty's face.

'What the hell are you talkin' about?'

'Nothing you'd understand.'

Ty gave him a perturbed frown, stared at the ground and shifted feet. He had something else on his mind, that was plain. It was the only thing that prevented him from questioning his brother's statement further.

'What're you chewin' on, Ty? Get out with it.'

Ty hesitated, sliding his jaw back and forth.

'I just been thinkin' maybe we should send Lacy on his way. He got Cleatus killed and all. Makes me wonder if he's really here to protect me or for somethin' else. I saw him talkin' to Pa yesterday. Didn't seem like Pa was too happy.'

Jep scoffed, sighed. 'He wouldn't be here at all if you'd keep your britches on.'

'What the hell's that s'posed to mean? You know that woman was lyin'.'

'Was she?' Jep had his doubts. It would be just like Ty to do something stupid like that. He'd met Kylie Barton and she just didn't impress him as the type to make up a story.

'Hell, you know she was! Whole town said so.' Ty's voice wavered and his eyes darted back and forth. Jep was damn near certain his brother was lying.

'Whole town or just a few Pa paid off to make sure?'

Crimson washed into Ty's face. 'I don't like you questioning my word, Jep. You best watch your damn mouth.'

Jep almost laughed. 'Any time you think you got the balls, Ty.'

Ty spat, eyed his brother with something close to hate, but made no move to take him on.

'That don't change the fact that Lacy might become a problem.'

'You're the one who agreed with sending Cleatus after that manhunter. Now Cleatus's dead.'

'More I think on it the more I think that was a mistake.'

'No foolin'?'

Ty ignored his brother's sarcasm. 'More I think on it the more I think Lacy might have been a-scared of that manhunter. That's why he didn't draw on him. And that's why he didn't want to go after him himself.'

Jep cocked an eyebrow. 'That just makes Lacy smarter than you, not a coward.'

'We best get rid of him, Jep.'

Jep shrugged. 'For once, little brother, I agree with you. I didn't want him here in the first place and the more I see of that *hombre*, the more hare-brained the notion to hire him becomes.'

'Then tell him to leave.'

Jep laughed. 'You brought him here by stepping out of line, you tell him to leave.'

'I will, Jep, I will. He don't scare me.'

'He oughta. Don't turn your back on him when you do.' Jep walked away from his brother. He agreed Lacy had to go and he would talk to his father about that, too. Meanwhile, despite what he told his brother about handling the job himself, he'd have to watch Ty's back. Blood was blood, no matter how stupid it was and Lacy was as vicious as any man Jep had encountered. He saw it in the man's dead eyes. There was nothing the man wasn't capable of, even murdering an innocent woman.

Lacy lingered at the corner of the veranda, keeping out of sight, listening to the tail end of the Galendez brothers' discussion regarding his deposition. He felt a measure of surprise that the younger one had the balls to bring up ousting him. He would have expected it out of Jep, but not Ty. Maybe it was simply sheer stupidly on the boy's part. The sonofabitch didn't appear to think before he acted. That was what got him in trouble with the Barton woman in the first place. Lacy had no doubt he'd done what the woman accused him of. Not that he cared a lick. It wasn't his concern. His concern was cash, lots of it, and he wasn't about to let anyone interfere with that, including the cattleman's sons.

He watched the older son walk away, leaving Ty standing there staring after him. A few moments later, Ty headed off in the direction of one of the corrals.

Lacy drifted away from the veranda, following the younger Galendez, keeping a careful eye that he wasn't observed doing so.

Ty kept going, rounding the corral and heading towards a tool-shed located a few hundred feet from the carriage-house. The boy was apparently intent on starting some chore.

Ty entered the tool-shed. Lacy glanced about, making certain no one would chance overseeing him. He entered the tool-shed behind Ty. His hand rested on the butt of his Smith & Wesson.

Ty turned when Lacy came in behind him, a startled look on his face quickly replaced with one of anger.

'Heard you been lookin' for me . . .' said Lacy. The little killer pulled the gun from its holster and kicked the door shut behind him.

CHAPTER SEVEN

Lead shattered a parlor window, sending sparkling diamonds of glass spiraling to the puncheon floor.

In the kitchen, John Deletéreo's heart jumped and he sprang from the hardbacked chair at the breakfast table, alarm flashing across his face. The chair toppled over backwards and his plate of bacon and eggs caught on his belt buckle as he leaped up, flipping over and splattering food across the table.

Sitting opposite him, Clarissa let out a small gasp, fear hardening the soft lines of her face. Her blue eyes widened and looked to him for an answer, one he feared to provide.

Something – some*one* – from his manhunting life had caught up with him.

His hand swept for the Peacemaker at his side as he flashed Clarissa a look.

'Stay here!' His tone came hard and demanding, but it was for her own good. 'Get under the table and stay away from the windows.'

She nodded, fear strengthening on her features. He cast her a final look, this time softer. She was beautiful, that woman. The sunlight streaming through the window gave her face a glow that told him he was the luckiest man in the world to have such a woman at his side. He had given up manhunting for her, decided to settle down in this log cabin atop a hillside west of the Pecos River. Raise a few cattle, maybe, create a life that didn't involve hardcases and nights alone on the trail. A life for them. She would have his child by harvest time, and he reckoned life couldn't have been any sweeter.

Until today.

Someone was out there, threatening all he had dreamed of and achieved, likely because some newspaper article had run a story on him retiring and pinpointed his location. He had enemies, too many to count, most unknown to him, hardcases looking to make a reputation or wanting to get even for justice delivered to one of their cronies.

The reason didn't matter. The threat was what counted. He wondered if there would ever come a day when he'd be allowed to live in peace.

He dashed from the room into the parlor, pausing for a second as he noted the glass sprinkled across the floor.

Another blast shattered the silence and a second window burst inward, glass shards lacerating the air, raining to the floor with the sound of skeletons dancing.

Then silence. He could hear the beating of his own heart, feel the throbbing of his pulse in his throat. He cut sideways and pressed himself against the heavy log wall beside the first window. He brought his Peacemaker up in front of his chest, finger feather-light on the trigger. Dampness coated his palms and his hand flexed on the ivory grip. An unusual thing for him, because normally he remained dead calm under a threat. But this time was different; this time he had everything to lose, a wife and an unborn child.

He chanced a look outside. The hillside, peppered with stands of cottonwood and piñon, appeared serene in the early-morning sunlight, emerald and aglow. Leaves swayed under a warm breeze; water sparkled from a trough. As if no danger impended, as if no shots had been fired. A lie. Because somewhere out there lurked a man with a gun who wanted nothing more than to end John Deletéreo's life.

Something moved. He caught just a glimpse of a figure scooting from one cottonwood to another, one with a thicker bole offering more protection.

John trigged a hasty shot, hoping to get lucky. The bullet chipped splinters off the cottonwood but missed the shooter.

The sniper was dressed in black clothing with a low-pulled hat and a bandanna covering most of his face. John had been unable to distinguish anything else about him, only that he was fairly large of build and surprisingly swift on his feet.

A shot rang out. Lead seared through the window opening, burying itself in the opposite wall.

John jumped back, pressing himself flat against the wall. The bullet had damn near taken his head off.

'Christ,' he muttered, sweat trickling down the side of his face, then shouted: 'Who are you?'

A laugh echoed back. 'I'm your death, manhunter!' The voice came muffled, raspy, its owner obviously attempting to disguise the tone. 'Got a nice fat contract on you, one thousand US greenbacks just to kill the most deadly manhunter this side of the Pecos. You should be honored, Mr John Dead.'

'Go to hell!' he shouted back, dread making his belly plunge. So that was it. His reputation had elicited a reward for his demise, despite his announced retirement.

Another shot answered. Lead thucked into the side of the house, near the window.

He whirled, straight-armed the Peacemaker through the opening and blasted three quick shots in the direction of the voice.

It was then that he saw there were two men, not one. With his gunfire he glimpsed a smaller fellow dressed the same way as the first jerk back behind a sheltering boulder.

At the same time the large man swung his gun out into the open and blasted a shot at John. It was hasty, ill-aimed but came damn close. The bullet dug a furrow across his cheek then plowed into a small table near the sofa. The bleeding gash stung like hell but was superficial.

Years of instinct guiding him, he swept his Peacemaker in a smooth arc towards the larger shooter, who had exposed himself just enough to fire.

John's finger tightened on the trigger.

The man jolted, staggered back a step, revealing himself further. The bullet had punched into his shoulder. He glanced down at the wound, forgetting for the moment where the shot had come from. An instant later, his head jerked up as he realized he presented a clear target. He tried to get his weapon up, but John blasted another shot. Lead stopped the man in his tracks and a rose of crimson bloomed on his chest.

John triggered another shot for good measure. The

bullet struck the man just above the bloody rose. The hardcase collapsed, going down face first and lying still in the morning sunlight.

A measure of satisfaction took him. One down, one left.

He drew back, plucking bullets from his belt and reloading.

'Come out and fight like a man, you sonofabitch!' he yelled, knowing it would do little good. Bushwhackers were all cowards. His only puzzle was why the first shot had taken out a window and effectively warned him that they were out there. Their ambush would have been a complete surprise otherwise. Had he stepped outside unaware of their presence, he would have been a dead man.

'I ain't your huckleberry, manhunter!' the man yelled back, voice still disguised.

John whirled and fired at the voice, but the bullet ricocheted harmlessly from the boulder.

It came a few seconds later. A sudden barrage of lead as the shooter lifted his gun above the boulder and triggered five shots towards the window.

John jumped back as he caught the glint of sunlight on the gun barrel, smiling to himself because the shooter had committed a useless move.

The smile dropped from his lips the instant he turned. The shooter had spotted what John saw now.

Clarissa, worry on her face, stepping into the parlor with a rifle. In doing so, she placed herself in a direct line with the window.

Three bullets drilled into her torso, each exploding in scarlet across her pink gingham dress. Her mouth dropped open. Shock and pain twisted her face. Blood snaked from the corner of her mouth.

The shots stopped.

She staggered a step forward, the rifle dropping from her fingers. It clattered on the floor and she fell a second behind it.

'Noooo!' he screamed, a sound torn from his heart, born of anguish. His protesting shrieks filled the room as he ran for her, fell beside her quivering body. 'Jesus . . . no . . .' His voice dropped to a whisper, and tears slipped from his eyes, dripping on to her dress.

'Please, Clarissa . . . don't leave . . .'

Her eyes tried to focus on him, glassy and blank.

'John . . . Johnny, help me . . . I can't feel . . . feel my . . .'

Her eyelids fluttered and her words drowned in a gurgle of blood that bubbled from her mouth. Her head fell back and she went limp in his arms. He tried to shake her back to life but it was a useless gesture.

He lowered her head gently to the floor, his hand shaking as it drifted over her eyelids, closing them.

She was gone. Everything he wanted, everything he cared about. Gone. Forever. Something in his heart shattered and grief surged in great gouts.

'Nooo . . .' The protest trickled into nothingness. He shook his head, at first slowly, then growing more violent and denying.

She couldn't be gone. She couldn't be . . .

He sprang to his feet, a surge of fury overwhelming his good sense. Fire filled his veins and he let out a primal scream torn from the depths of his soul. His hand tightened on the Peacemaker, going white.

Whirling, he stared at the door, lips quivering, breath stuttering.

He ran for the door then, gouting emotion driving him, a crimson haze before his eyes.

He threw the heavy log door open, casting away all caution with it.

He stormed across the porch and out into the yard. His Peacemaker came up, finger spasming on the trigger as he strode towards the boulder behind which the shooter remained hidden.

He didn't care any more. The world had nothing left for him without Clarissa. His life was over.

Bullets chipped stone and blue smoke billowed in the air, its scent acrid in his nostrils.

Then it was over. The hammer clacked on an empty chamber.

Deafening silence rang in his ears, but only for a moment.

A man stepped out from behind the boulder and triggered three shots. The first plowed through John's side. The second entered his chest as he was half-turned, staggering back from the first's impact. A third dug a gory chasm across his belly, but didn't enter.

He went down hard on his back, gaze flung up at a sapphire sky. A hawk drifted overhead, strangely surreal, and for a moment Clarissa's face superimposed on the blue, then dissolved in a blood-colored explosion of raindrops.

A dark face filled his sight, the bandit kneeling over him, peering at his eyes. He couldn't tell anything about the man's face; the bandanna was pulled too high, his vision too blurred even to make out the eyes.

'You won't make it . . .' the man said, voice raspy, still disguised. 'I should thank you though for saving me the trouble of killing Hascal over there. He damn near blew the whole thing firing at shadows.'

'Bas . . . bastard . . .' John muttered as the man's face waverd in and out, everything shimmering and fuzzy.

'Goodbye, manhunter. I told you I wouldn't be your huckleberry.' The man stood and kicked John in the face. John barely felt the blow because darkness swarmed over him.

He sprang bolt upright in bed, heart pounding and sweat pouring from his body despite the coolness of the hotel room. His gasping breath burned in his throat and tremors shook him for several moments. Burying his face in his hands, he fought the surging grief that always came with the nightmare.

Two years ago. Clarissa died at the hand of an unknown gunman.

Two years ago, a man named John Deletéreo died as well.

Face lifting from his hands, he threw off the blanket tangled about his legs and sat on the edge of the bed. His fingers drifted to the scar at his chest, then to the one at his side.

Two bullets had entered. One had gone clean out the back, doing little damage really, missing any vital organs. The second in the chest . . . that one had nearly done the job, by all rights should have.

He'd forgotten that he ordered supplies the day before and that the shopkeeper had offered to bring them out to the cabin. The man was a friend of Clarissa's, a cousin, if he recollected right. Had the man shown up fifteen minutes earlier he would have been lying dead with

Clarissa. John Deletéreo would have bled to death in the grass.

The shopkeeper managed to get him into the back of the wagon and drive him to the doc's. Even then his life hung by a thread for months. The bullet had missed his heart but shattered a rib and lodged near his spine. The doc removed it but fever set in and only by some quirk of a merciless God had John Deletéreo survived.

They told everyone he'd died that day, printing it in the newspaper and detailing how two graves rested up on the hillside. In truth he had died. All he was perished with Clarissa, leaving a husk filled with grief and bitterness, no real direction. Why he went on living, what pulled him through, he didn't know. He visited Clarissa's grave before leaving their home completely, never to return. The second grave, the one with his marker, lay empty. The shopkeep saw to the disposal of the hardcase's body, a man named Hascal, whose face John had never seen until the doc brought a Wanted dodger that branded him a murderer many times over.

The second attacker made a clean getaway. John was forced to give up searching for him after many wasted months. No way to track a masked killer who vanished into the countryside.

Rumors swirled around John Deletéreo beyond that point. Folks saw him and reported it, turned him into a ghost who rode the dark reaches of the Western night, delivering grim justice to the guilty. He became the stuff of legend and camp-fire tales.

He remained the West's most deadly manhunter, now more dangerous dead than when he was alive. That was what the stories said.

They were likely right.

He missed her. Lord, how he missed her. The dream brought her face back in stark detail and he relived her death each time with the same intensity as the day it happened.

He stood suddenly, fury and grief raging inside him. He swept the basin and pitcher from the bureau top with an angry lash of his hand. They shattered against the wall and fell in shards to the dirty floorboards.

He fell against the bureau, tears welling, emotion raging. Christ, it would never be over. How could it be with that sonofabitch out there? How could he ever find even the smallest measure of peace? How could a dead man ever live again?

Kylie Barton stared out through the window at the encroaching dawn. She'd spent most of the night awake, afraid of shadows, startled by every little noise. The new day brought little hope, though at least she had her money back and soon would leave this place. Nothing remained for her here, but she couldn't force away the feeling that she'd failed somehow, that she'd simply given up. Ty Galendez would live free, never paying for his transgressions, his crimes, while she would go on living with nightmares. Soiled.

You could go to that man, John, tell him what happened. Maybe he can help. . . .

The thought had entered her head more than once since his visit the other morning. Twice she'd found herself close to riding to town to ask his help. Something told her she could trust him, that he was unlike any other man. The gypsy in her wasn't dead, she realized, merely frightened. She could still read men, could read him. And in him she saw pain and loss and a longing for something unknown, perhaps unobtainable. Why had he come to a hell-hole like Payton's Bluff? She didn't know, but he had offered his help and that made him better than anyone else in that god-forsaken place.

So why don't you take him up on his offer? she asked herself. Why don't you go to him?

She honestly didn't know. She only knew she was scared, hopeless, and felt the need to run from her life, from her past, from everything and everyone associated with Payton's Bluff.

She glanced behind her at the portmanteau packed and waiting in the corner. She couldn't take everything, but with the money she would have enough to start over somewhere. Maybe back East, where memories couldn't find her.

He could help you . . .

She turned back to the window. The sun now peeked above the horizon, painting the sky with rose and orange. Confusion gripped her, making her unsure of her decision for no reason she could place – or perhaps admit to herself.

He intrigued her, the way no man had since her husband's death. Sometimes a body just knew when something existed between itself and another.

Movement startled her. A shadow, slipping across the yard to a tree, vanishing.

Had she really seen anything? Or was it simply fear causing her to imagine ghosts?

A shiver went through her and she moved away from the window. Her heart began to beat faster, harder, and tightness clamped about her chest.

She hurried over to the Winchester resting on wall pegs and lifted it from its mount. The weapon felt heavy, comforting in her grip. It was loaded. She'd kept it loaded ever since that night in September.

She turned and stared at the door, indecision gripping her. Was she just being foolish? It could have been a bear or some other large animal.

No, the shape wasn't right. It was a man.

What man would be around here at such an ungodly hour of day? She had to be wrong, was letting fear get the better of her nerves.

But she couldn't shake the feeling that someone was out there. She stepped to the door, easing back the bolt and turning the handle, keeping the Winchester close to her chest.

She let the door swing inward and a chilly autumn breeze swept through, making her shudder. She stared out into the brightening morning, a time when gory splashes of light cavorted with fleeing shadows and gave the day a picturesque quality that normally highlighted the beauty in the world, yet now somehow only accentuated the menace.

Refusing to give in to fear this time, she stepped outside on to the porch, gaze sweeping left then right. Nothing. No sign of life or movement.

She eased down the steps and moved towards where she thought she glimpsed the shape behind the tree. On reaching the tree she discovered nothing there and let out a relieved sigh. She had been imagining things after all.

'You're jumping at spooks,' she assured herself, relaxing her grip a bit on the Winchester.

Something hit the back of her head then, something solid that caused an explosive ringing in her skull.

She fell forward, the Winchester tumbling from her grip. Her face hit the partially frozen ground and for moments her head reeled. She wasn't sure she hadn't blacked out because when her vision cleared boots stood before her.

Terror rushed back in and, letting out a strangled sound, she struggled to get to her feet.

A fist clipped her in the jaw, sending her reeling over onto her back, stunned.

'Just came to get my money back, missy,' said the man standing over her.

Eyes focusing, she saw him then, the little bastard she'd called upon herself.

'Get the hell off my land!' She spat the words, anger mixing with fear.

He laughed, a mocking sound that rang in her ears like Lucifer's compassion.

'I will, missy, but just wanted to visit you a last time before your hangin'.'

She peered at him, a measure of puzzlement coming onto her features.

'What the devil are you talking about?'

He shrugged. 'Reckon you'll find that out later.'

He was atop her then, hands foraging in her skirt pockets and violating her body. He pulled out the folded greenbacks and stood again, tucking them into his shirt pocket.

'Canceled your refund . . .' The snake smile slithered onto his lips. He picked up her Winchester and examined it. 'Think I'll hold onto this. Young gal like you – who knows what fool notion you might get in your head. Might even decide to kill poor Ty Galendez yourself.' Something lay behind his words. She heard it in his voice but couldn't identify what it was.

He backed away, then turned and walked towards the trail. She watched him go, utter defeat washing over her. She had nothing left. He'd taken her money and with it any hope of her leaving, running. He'd come to taunt her, gloat over some dark scheme known only to him. He thrived on that. But it didn't matter, because the last spark of strength flickered out in her. Curling into a ball, she lay on the cold ground, sobbing, tears surging, wishing the little bastard had been merciful enough to kill her.

CHAPTER EIGHT

John Deletéreo stared out through his hotel room window, pondering his future. He had gained what he came for: an introduction to Payton Galendez and for all intents confirmation of the facts laid down in his mother's last letter to him. The letter lay on the bed, opened.

A bitter sense of anticlimax gripped him, but he honestly hadn't expected much better from Galendez. The man claimed no ties to his past indiscretions, wanted no responsibility for a woman who had spent far too much of her life suffering.

He wished he could say it surprised him. Men like Payton Galendez considered themselves above common folk, better, least they got to thinking that way after they'd forged their empires. Emma Blake was a poor woman, one who had slaved every day of her life and never had much to show for it, except for a son in whom she instilled a moral code that saw others punished for their crimes. Payton Galendez wouldn't shed a tear for either. He belonged to another world, one that had no room for a bastard son named John.

He went to the bed, sat on the edge, his heart heavy.

Picking up the letter, he reread it for the hundredth time in the past two weeks:

> *My son,*
> *If you are reading this letter then my time here on earth is ended. I am sorry I couldn't give you more than this simple goodbye. You turned out better than I could have hoped, despite the many mistakes I made. You should have the truth about me. I hope it sets your mind at peace. I trust in the man you have become. I know you will use the knowledge as it best suits you.*
>
> *Your true father left the day he found out I was with child. He had plans, hopes, dreams he refused to abandon. Those plans had no room for an unwed woman and a baby. He left and never looked back. He told me that if I ever spoke the truth about what happened, his taking me before vows and against my will, he would see to it you were taken from me. I could not live with that so I never told a soul about him. As the years went by the memory faded, the pain lessened. You grew and somehow it no longer seemed so important, because despite what he did to me, he also left me with a precious gift.*
>
> *That man was your father. I have no doubt you will recognize his name. I also have no doubt you will forgive him, as I have in my final days. That man's name is Payton Galendez . . .*

The letter went on, telling him how much she loved him and prayed that his life would be better, but his eyes grew moist with tears he wouldn't let fall and the words blurred. He folded the paper and tucked it back into the envelope, then stood.

Payton Galendez, his real father. Ty and Jep his half-brothers. John was heir to a fortune if he could prove paternity, but he didn't care to try. He had no need of the money, anyway, but all his life he had burned with the desire to know who he truly was, where he came from. Now he did and it provided not a lick of satisfaction.

In fact, it left him with nothing more than the empty life he'd been living since Clarissa's death. He would ride out as he had ridden in. Alone. None the richer, none the wiser. He'd mined fool's gold.

A knock sounded on his hotel room door, jolting him from his thoughts. He stared at the door a moment, hand instinctively settling on the butt of his Peacemaker.

He went to the door and stood to the side as he drew it open. His hand relaxed and he let out the breath he'd been holding.

Kylie Barton stood in the hallway, her head lowered. She looked up at him, pain in her reddened eyes, her bottom lip swollen further.

'Miss Barton . . .' He raised an eyebrow.

'You . . . you said if I wanted to talk, I could come to you. If I needed help . . .'

He nodded. 'Somethin' happened?'

She gave a quick nod. 'Can we go somewhere. Wouldn't be proper for a woman to be alone with you in your room, would it?' She said it oddly, as if she'd lost the ability to distinguish between right and wrong for the moment. Her eyes had a slightly dazed look.

He went to the bedpost and grabbed his Stetson, set it on his head. He returned to the door and took her by the elbow, closed his door, then guided her down the dingy hallway.

He walked her towards the café where he had break-fasted. From the corner of his eye he noticed folks on the street casting them peculiar looks, expressions filled with . . . what? Blame? Accusation? Kylie avoided their looks, kept her head down.

A woman passed by, swiveled her head and spat at the young woman. Kylie ignored it, simply wiping the folds of her skirt together.

'What the hell's wrong with you?' John sent the woman an angry glare.

The woman sneered. 'She's worse than a whore, mister. She ain't wanted in this town. You ain't neither if you take up with that hussy!' The woman spun and trotted off.

'What the hell is she talkin' about?' he asked Kylie, who gave him a guilty expression.

'I'm sorry, I didn't mean to bring my problems down on you.'

He shook his head, his blood racing. He had no toler-ance for pious types who criticized others when likely their own pantries were stacked with sin.

'Everyone in town treat you that way?'

'No, the general store owner brings me supplies. He's a kindly man. A few others who don't quite take to the Galendez boys, 'specially one of them, treat me well.'

'I reckon a mean-tempered fella like Ty has his share of enemies.'

She looked at him, appearing suddenly fragile and shades paler.

'You . . . know him?'

'Met him at the saloon the first night I rode in. He was sitting with Lacy and Jep. Ain't much between him and a bullet.'

'How much did Lacy tell you?'

They reached the café and he opened the door for her. A waitress cast her a disgusted look and John returned it with a look of his own that said he'd brook no insult. He motioned for a coffee-pot as he guided Kylie to a back table. The waitress reluctantly brought the pot, along with two cups. She gave Kylie a look of contempt as she walked away.

He poured the coffee and she clutched the cup in both hands, fingers draining white. She remained silent, as if having trouble gathering her thoughts.

He gave her time, setting his Stetson on the seat next to him. The place was nearly empty, too late for the lunch crowd and too early for supper business.

He peered at her, saw hopelessness clouding her amethyst eyes. Likely she was still distrusting but desperation had brought her here. He'd have one chance at gaining her faith, so he decided direct was the best way.

'Lacy showed me the telegram you sent summoning him here.'

She met his gaze and no deception showed in her eyes, just honest emotion.

'I sent for him. It was a foolish thing to do. I wanted him to kill a man for me.'

He nodded. 'Ty Galendez.'

'I wanted him dead. I reckon I still might.' Bitterness laced her tone, but along with it a measure of relief. She'd likely been carrying a load of guilt and telling him lifted some of the burden.

'Callin' a man like Lacy . . .' He kept any hint of reprimand out of his voice. She didn't need scolding. Likely she had berated herself over it a hundred times worse than anyone else could.

'I know. I made a mistake. He's an evil man, John.'

'You seen him again since that night?'

She nodded. 'He came early this morning. Took back the money you returned. He hit me, stole my rifle. Acted like he knew something was going to happen, but he didn't say what. I got more scared. I didn't know what to do.'

Her words sent a tingle of alarm through him. He reckoned Lacy didn't do anything without a reason, one that meant harm for another.

'Why d'you want Galendez dead?'

She swallowed hard, eyes growing glassy with tears.

'He courted me for a spell. I made it plain I wasn't interested. He's young, hotheaded. It might have meant an easy life for me but I couldn't abide his temper and his . . .'

'His what?'

'His pressing me to do something I had no interest in.' Her face reddened and he wasn't sure whether it came from embarrassment or anger.

'This something you're talkin' about, what—'

'He took it,' she cut in. 'He took it.' A tear slipped down her face. 'I used to walk, late at night sometimes. Along the trail. I liked to clear my head that way. He was waitin' for me . . . he'd been drinking.' She sniffled, a shudder rattling through her.

His brow knotted. 'What are you sayin', ma'am?'

'He raped me.' Her voice climbed a notch in pitch. 'That's why I wanted him dead. I know it was wrong but I didn't know what else to do.'

The revelation made his blood race. He felt inclined to kill Ty Galendez himself, even if they were blood relations.

'You told the marshal?'

She nodded, swiping tears from her face with the back of her hand.

'He refused to do anything about it because it was a Galendez. I told others but they all stood up for Ty and his family. They called me a liar. Marshal made a pretense of talkin' to Ty but it was just a big joke to them. They said a gal should just shut her mouth and consider herself lucky a Galendez would even bother with a no-good dressmaker. I was beneath his station. Soon folks started lookin' at me like I was something filthy. They told me I would no longer be let near the children, told me to stay away from town. A few took pity on me, like I said. I was savin' to start over somewhere else, but Lacy has my money now.'

John struggled to keep his own anger from overwhelming him. He believed her story; he saw honest emotion in her eyes, heard it in her voice. The old man had passed down some bad stock to his son. Only this woman had tried taking justice into her own hands, unlike his own mother, who had let the elder Galendez simply ride away and start another life.

'How'd you learn about a man like Lacy in the first place?' He placed his hand over hers. She clutched his fingers, looked up at him, teary-eyed.

'A man named Sutter. I went to him, knowing he could find me someone. Ain't no secret he'll find you whatever you want in this town if you give him a bottle and money. He gave me an address, said a telegram would get to Lacy there. A relative of his, I think, who passed notes to him.'

John nodded. 'Reckon I can put the rest together. This man Sutter played both ends, likely went to someone, maybe one of the Galendezes, maybe someone loyal to them. Whoever it was wired Lacy's relative and offered to pay him more than you ever could. Men like Lacy are bought easy enough.'

'I don't understand why he still came. He could have taken the money and never showed up.'

'He wanted your money, too, plus I'm willin' to bet Galendez wanted to throw a scare into you so you'd never pull a stunt like that again.'

'Why's he still here, then?'

He uttered a chopped laugh. 'Men like Lacy ain't so easy to get rid of once they get the scent of green. He's got his reason, I reckon. Maybe Galendez got more than he bargained for.'

She searched his eyes, her fingers tightening a bit on his hand.

'You believe me?'

'Got no reason not to.'

'No one in this town would. What makes you take the word of someone who lied to you when you tried to help her?'

He offered a thin smile. 'I came to this town looking for Payton Galendez. My mother passed on two weeks ago, but she left me a note. I never knew who my father was till I read it. Seems takin' things that don't belong to them runs in the Galendez blood.'

'But that makes Payton Galendez—'

'My father.' He nodded, face turning grim. 'He ain't the man I thought he would be. He's just a gilded cowchip.'

Relief flooded her features. Her eyelids fluttered.

'Thank you for believing me . . . John. I can't tell you how alone I felt having a whole town callin' me a liar.'

'I'll get your money back, ma'am. I reckon a man like

Lacy's got a warrant on him somewhere. I'll ride to the county marshal and see what I can find, so I got legal grounds to bring him in. I'll see what I can do about Ty Galendez too, but I'm afraid I can't make any promises there. Payton's a powerful man and it will still be your word against his son's and this town.'

She looked at the table, sadness etching deep lines into her face.

'I . . . can't afford to pay you. Even if you got the money back I would have barely enough to leave, so it ain't worth risking your life for.'

'I made you a promise. I aim to keep it.' He gave her a warm smile, one she returned. 'And maybe my motives ain't all unselfish. I reckon I'd welcome spendin' more time with you. Best you ride with me to fetch that warrant. Won't be safe here with whatever Lacy's got in mind. I'll make sure your propriety's not in question.'

She laughed without humor. 'I'm a tainted woman. Might be your propriety that's at stake.'

The café door opened before he could say anything further. His gaze swung in that direction. Two men stepped into the eatery: Marshal Studdard and Lacy. Both had guns drawn and he saw the lawdog scanning the place, then pointing a finger towards them. Someone had tipped them off that he and Kylie were here, but what the devil did they want?

The lawdog came around the table and Lacy kept his gun leveled on John. For a moment John wasn't entirely sure that the boyish killer wasn't just going to pull the trigger. Something in the little man's eyes wanted him dead then and there.

John pulled his hand from Kylie's and slid it to the edge

of the table. Lacy wasn't going to find him easy prey if he made a move.

'Keep your hands where I can see them, Deletéreo.' The marshal gestured with his gun.

'What's the meaning of this, Marshal?' John asked, gaze flicking to Lacy, who grinned like a dog who'd just swallowed a steak dinner.

The marshal turned to Kylie.

'Please come with us, ma'am. I'm placin' you under arrest.'

'On what charge?' John asked, suspicion welling inside him.

'Murder, Mr Deletéreo. This here young woman killed Ty Galendez.'

Kylie let out a small gasp and John's eyes narrowed.

'I'll go with you.' He started to get up.

'No sir, you won't.' The marshal motioned for Kylie to stand. 'You want to see her again you come to the saloon at three. We got a counsel all set to hear the story and pronounce sentence.'

The marshal took the young woman by the arm and led her from the café. Lacy lingered behind a moment, grin stuck to his lips, gun still aimed at John.

The manhunter's gaze locked with the little killer's.

'You had something to do with this, Lacy. I'll see you hang.'

Lacy gave a small laugh. 'You ain't so mighty now when it's me holdin' the gun, are you, manhunter? Maybe you'd like to make me the same offer you did in the saloon the other night?'

John's eyes darkened. 'That really what you want to see happen?'

Lacy peered at him, seemed to lose his nerve. The smile faded and he backed from the café, closing the door behind him.

Three o'clock. That gave him only a half-hour. John had no doubt that any trial would be a mockery. They'd decided to move on Kylie Barton and silence her for good. For one of the few times in his life he had no idea what the hell his next move would be if he were going to save her.

John Deletéreo walked into the saloon five minutes before three. Tables had been pushed together in a horseshoe pattern and men sat at each. At the first table were Jep and Payton Galendez, both of them somber-faced, with dark pouches nesting beneath their eyes. They glanced at John as he stepped through the batwings but quickly averted their gazes. The man sitting beside them was unfamiliar, but John assumed it was he who would state the case against Kylie Barton. The fellow was slight, with a protruding Adam's apple and receding hairline. His suit had seen better days and his hand shook slightly as he checked the watch dangling from a chain slung from his vest pocket.

Kylie sat at another table, face pale, drawn, defeat welded onto her features. She knew they had set her up and the conclusion to this mock trial could have only one outcome. Beside her sat a balding plump fellow wearing spectacles, likely a lawyer for her defense, one paid from deep Galendez pockets, if John read the situation right.

Lacy sat in the front at another table, next to the marshal. His eyes followed John as the manhunter stepped down into the saloon proper and selected a chair. He cast the little killer a dark look that promised they'd finish their business at some point in the near future.

126

A handful of bargirls lounged at the back of the saloon, leaning over tables and watching the proceedings with little interest. A few other men sat around, none of them familiar to John, but likely townsfolk friendly to the Galendez family hired to serve as witnesses to the proceedings.

'If everyone's present, we will proceed,' the marshal said. 'I'll be judging the proceedings and pronouncing sentence . . . should one be necessary.' His emphasis on the last part of the sentence made it plain one damn sure would be. John had half an urge to shoot the man where he sat. He didn't know who was worse at the moment, Lacy, an outright killer, or the marshal, a crooked lawdog who justified cold-blooded murder under the guise of the law.

'Call your first witness, Mr Cowell.'

Cowell, the man sitting with the Galendezes, stood and motioned to Lacy, who rose and moved to a seat across from the marshal at the same table.

'You swear to tell the truth, the whole truth?' the marshal asked.

Lacy made no attempt to hide the snake smile that crossed his lips.

'I do, Marshal.'

Cowell stood before Lacy, face serious, playing his role to the hilt. He made a spectacle of clearing his throat.

'Mr Lacy, would you please tell the counsel why you came to Payton's Bluff.'

Lacy cast the man a surly look.

'Thought I told you not to call me mister.'

Cowell licked his lips and took a step back.

'Please proceed with your story, er, Lacy.'

Lacy glanced at Kylie, his eyes unreadable.

'I received a telegram askin' me here to kill a man.'

Cowell nodded. 'I see. And who was this man you were summoned to kill in cold blood?'

'His name was Ty Galendez, the poor boy who was found murdered in the tool-shed.'

'Were you offered a sum of money to perform this duty, sir?' Cowell's tone became grave. His features drew into intense lines and he fingered his watch-chain.

'Yes, sir, I most certainly was. It plain disgusted me, it did. I was shocked someone would go to that measure.'

John's belly twisted. Lacy was a damn poor liar, but it made no difference to the assembled company, with the possible exception of Jep, whose face registered contempt at Lacy's statement. The boy quickly hid the expression, his features going back to solemn lines of grief.

'And what did you do when you received this telegram, sir?' Cowell rubbed his chin in a scholarly manner, not bothering to look directly at Lacy when he asked the question. John reckoned Cowell had gotten his mannerisms out of some pulp novel court scene.

'Why, what any decent folk would do, my good man. I sent a warning to Payton Galendez and rode out here as fast I could to prevent a tragedy. Reckon I failed in my duty, though.' Lacy hung his head, as if in deep regret. The act might have been funny under less serious circumstances. John's dislike for the little killer strengthened by the moment. Cowell cleared his throat again.

'And the person who sought to hire you for this dastardly mission, is that person here in this room?'

Lacy's head came up. 'Why, yes, she most assuredly is.'

'Would you care to point her out for the counsel, er, Lacy?'

Lacy's gaze flicked to Kylie Barton and he raised a finger.

'She's sitting right there, sir. Miss Kylie Barton. She's the one who wanted Ty Galendez dead.'

Cowell's face took on the appropriate amount of shock.

'Do you have proof of this accusation, sir?'

'I most certainly do. I would never presume to ruin a woman's fine reputation without substantial evidence that she had committed wrongdoing.' Lacy fished in a pocket and drew out a yellow slip of paper. He passed it across the table to the marshal.

The marshal opened the folded telegram and scanned the lines.

'Plain as day. This here telegram states conclusively that Miss Barton requested the services of Lacy for a killin', the murder of Ty Galendez.'

Cowell nodded somberly. 'Thank you, that will be all, um, Lacy.'

The lawdog's gaze swept to the man sitting beside Kylie. 'Your witness, Butler.'

The plump man looked up over his wire-rimmed spectacles and shook his head. 'No questions, your honor.'

John's belly plunged, though he'd expected little better. The young woman had no defense, but the charade went beyond even what he figured it would. His gaze centered on the Galendez men. Payton stared straight ahead, unflinching, but Jep's gaze followed Lacy as the killer returned to his side of table. The accusation in the young man's eyes appeared stronger now, but vanished the next instant when Cowell called him to the witness table.

Jep Galendez sat himself and answered yes to the

marshal's flat swear-to-tell-the-truth question.

'Who found the body of your brother, Mr Galendez?' Cowell asked, leaning his thigh against the table.

'I did.' Jep's voice came low.

'You discovered it in the tool-shed, did you not?'

'Objection, leading the witness,' mumbled Butler, not bothering to look up.

Cowell made a waving motion with his hand.

'I withdraw the question.' He returned his attention to Jep. 'Where did you discover your brother's body, Mr Galendez?'

Jep sighed, eyes glossing with moisture.

'In the tool-shed, sir.'

'How had your brother met with his unfortunate end?'

'He was shot, once, though the chest.'

'Did you at any time hear a gunshot?'

'Yes, I heard a shot. I wasn't close, though. Took me time to reach the shed.'

'Did you see anyone near the tool-shed?'

Jep started to squirm at the question, eyes darting. Finally he answered.

'No, no one . . .'

John studied the Galendez boy closely. He was leaving out something and was damned uncomfortable doing it.

Cowell pushed away from the table and walked to a chair. He lifted a rifle tagged with a slip of paper.

'I wish to submit Exhibit A, Marshal.' He placed the rifle on the table in front of the lawman. 'This rifle was located near the tool-shed. I reckon it belongs to Miss Barton.'

The marshal's gaze turned to Kylie, whose face was bloodless and who was twisting her fingers into knots.

'That true, Miss Barton? This your rifle?'

Her eyes widened, but she nodded.

'Yes, it's mine. Lacy stole it from me.'

Cowell uttered a short laugh.

'I'm sure he did, Miss Barton. I'm sure he did. With your reputation for lying, I might have your counsel advise you not to go beyond yes or no answers. Just a piece of friendly advice.' Cowell offered a smug expression.

John shook his head in disgust. He reckoned no one had bothered matching the bullet in Ty's body with one from the rifle, nor would they. He was willing to wager they came from two different sources but it didn't matter to anyone here. No one would bother to question the stupidity of her leaving the rifle handy as evidence against herself, either. The cell door was already slammed shut and locked.

'Do you wish to cross-examine Mr Galendez, Butler?' the marshal asked.

'No questions, sir,' Butler said, voice low.

'Do you wish to call your own witnesses, Mr Butler?'

Butler shook his head. 'No witnesses, your honor.'

'Then I reckon I've seen enough,' Marshal Studdard said. 'I pronounce Miss Barton guilty of the crime of murder. It's clear she had intent all along to bring about Ty Galendez's death and accomplished that plan with her own rifle. I thereby sentence her to hang by the neck until dead soon as a gallows can be built.'

As if in response to the pronouncement, hammering echoed from outside the saloon. Each bang thundered through John's nerves like a gunshot.

The marshal stood, as did Lacy, both men drawing guns. Both counsel proceeded to leave the saloon while

Lacy and Studdard helped Kylie from her seat and guided her out of the barroom.

Payton and Jep Galendez stood next, John rising to his feet a beat behind them. Payton cast John a dark look as he passed. The young Galendez stopped a moment, looking as if he wanted to say something but thinking better of it.

'You know this ain't right, Jep.' John locked gazes with the boy.

'I . . . I'm sorry, Mr Deletéreo. I can't do anything about it.' With that he left the bar.

John pushed through the batwings and walked out onto the boardwalk. He spotted the marshal and Lacy standing with Kylie twenty feet away, observing men who'd begun work constructing a gallows from boards lying in the back of a wagon. He reckoned they'd waste no time in silencing Kylie Barton for good.

The marshal cast John a look, a ghost of a smile on his face.

'Go back to wherever you came from, Deletéreo,' he shouted. 'This town don't want you here. Longer you stay the more likely it is that gallows will get plenty of use.'

The marshal turned, guiding Kylie towards his office. Lacy followed after throwing a glance backward at John.

John couldn't recollect a time he'd ever felt quite as helpless as he did now.

CHAPTER NINE

Marshal Studdard locked Kylie Barton in one of the three cells in his office. He made sure she had a window that faced the workers building her gallows. A twinge of guilt took him – she was innocent, after all – but it wasn't enough to sway his decision. He couldn't risk her hiring anyone else to cause trouble and there was the matter of Ty Galendez's murder.

His gaze focused on Lacy, who leaned a shoulder against the wall next to the window and folded his arms. A smug expression turned the little bastard's lips and Studdard knew damn well he had arranged Ty's killing. Studdard wondered if that had been such a good idea. They could have found another way to keep the Barton woman quiet. Now Deletéreo might prove a bigger risk and Studdard had no desire to get on Payton Galendez's bad side, either. Surely the cattleman didn't believe the Barton woman had killed his son.

He went to his desk, throwing one last glance at Kylie Barton, whose face looked three shades paler as she sat on the bunk and stared at the floor. A frown turned his lips and worry creased his forehead.

'Second thoughts, Studdard?'

He looked over to see Lacy studying at him, reading his face perfectly.

'You sure you know what you're doin'? Takin' a hell of a risk, ain't we?'

'I'm sure I have no idea what you are talkin' about, Marshal. I just did my sworn duty testifying against a murderess.'

Studdard's expression turned to one of sarcastic disbelief.

'I ain't a fool, Lacy. I know damn well what happened to that Galendez boy. You best hope his pa don't take the same notion.'

Lacy grinned. 'Reckon he already has, but he won't raise a hand against me while I got enough to ruin him.'

'Yeah? Whatta you got? Just what I gave you and with Ty dead it might not make such a difference to the old man. He ain't the type to be under anyone's thumb for long.'

Lacy shrugged. 'All men got their breaking-points, Studdard. Even Galendez. I'm sure he wouldn't want to lose a second son.' The threat behind his voice came cold and clear.

'You got it all figured out, don't you?' Studdard's tone held a note mockery. Lacy's expression chilled.

'Best watch your tongue, Studdard. Hell of a lot more money in this to split one way 'stead of two.'

Studdard considered it, feeling a shiver threaten to run up his spine. Lacy wasn't one to be trifled with; no matter how much guilt he might feel over the Barton woman he had to admit with a measure of shame he was afraid of the little killer. He'd seen far too much of the man's cold-blooded conscience when they worked together not to be.

'What about Deletéreo? The woman was with him. She might have told him everything. What if he brings in the county marshal?'

'He won't leave her long enough to do that. You know that, don't you?'

The marshal shrugged, little conviction in his expression.

'Maybe he will. I told him to go.'

Lacy let out a scoffing laugh. 'You see the way he looked at that woman?' Lacy ducked his chin towards the jail. Kylie's eyes centered on the little killer, defiant, filled with fury. 'He's got it for her, even if he don't know it yet. That's the way to get to him, his weakness.'

'How do you know that?' Studdard cast him a skeptical expression. Lacy turned to look out the window.

'I just know. He won't leave without her. Just a matter of time before he comes and it won't matter if it's legal. He'll break her out until he can figure out how to clear her name.'

'I don't see it. He'll just move on.' Studdard wished he believed his own words. But he didn't. Lacy was dead right and that was that. Lacy shook his head.

'You're a piss-poor marshal, Studdard, and an even worse judge of character. Deletéreo needs to be dealt with and I aim to do just that.'

'When?' Studdard shifted in his seat, fidgeted with a sheet of paper on his desk by folding over a corner.

'Sooner the better. Fact, just a few minutes from now.'

'What you got in mind?' He didn't care for the look on Lacy's face. It boded ill, not just for the manhunter but for himself as well.

'You get out to the Sutter place. Keep hidden until a bit

after that manhunter shows up and goes in. Then just do your duty.'

'My duty?'

'Mr Deletéreo's a murderer, Marshal. Letter of the law's clear on that. 'Sides, poor Cleatus needs to rest in peace, too. Reckon he can't do that with his killer runnin' around loose.'

'You want me to arrest him?'

'Miss Barton needs company for her hangin', don't you think?'

Worried lines etched Studdard's face. He shook his head.

'I don't like this, that manhunter's—'

'Just a man, Studdard. Pick your balls up off the floor and do your job.'

Studdard didn't care for it one bit. But he reckoned he was more afraid of Lacy than of Deletéreo. Now that the kick-backs he got from Ty were gone, blackmailing Payton Galendez was about the only option if Studdard intended to keep the payments coming in, and Lacy was a conduit to that.

'Where will you be?'

Lacy gave his snake smile. 'Out at the Galendez place. Reckon the old man won't want to miss seeing his son hang.'

Studdard's brow furrowed. 'His son? Jep ain't hangin'.'

Lacy chuckled. 'No, *he* ain't, is he? But John Deletéreo will be.'

'What the hell are you talkin' about, Lacy?' Studdard didn't understand a word of it and didn't really care to. The little killer had finally flipped his saddle.

Lacy ignored the question, casting a last look at the cell. Kylie Barton still stared at him. He tipped his finger to his hat, before walking out the door.

The marshal sat in his chair, a wave of coldness washing through his being, his better judgment rebelling against Lacy's orders. But too many years of milking the golden cow overpowered conscience.

He stood, flashed Kylie a glance, then headed out.

The saloon was crowded again now that the trial was over. Cowboys had gotten an early start on the night's festivities.

Lacy walked through the batwings, stopped and peered about. He scanned the patrons and bargirls until he located the girl he wanted, the blonde he'd chased out of the room in which he'd killed Sutter. Wearing a blue sateen bodice, she leaned over a cowboy, displaying her ample charms next to his cheek.

Lacy threaded his way through the tables to her and clamped a hand about her arm.

'Hey – what the hell do you think—' Her voice dropped off suddenly, as she looked into the eyes of the man who had grabbed her. Fear danced in her dull gaze.

Lacy dragged her away from the table, the cowboy too far in his cups to care. He hauled her over to the stairway leading to the upper level, out of earshot of other girls and customers.

'You're gonna do me a little favor, missy.' Lacy's tone brooked no objection. She looked at him as if considering crying out for help or telling him to go to hell but fear overpowered any resistance.

'What kinda favor?'

'You're gonna deliver an important message for me to a fella at the hotel. Find out from the clerk which room he's in.'

'What kind of message?' Suspicion invaded her tone.

'Here's what you'll tell him.' Lacy whispered it into her ear. 'Make sure you're convincing or you won't be in any condition to earn a living with your ass ever again.'

She looked plainly unenthused with the idea but he knew she'd do what he'd told her to do. He reached into a pocket and drew out a bill, then stuffed it into the top of her bodice between her breasts.

John Delétéreo's belly twisted the more he dwelled on the mock trial and Kylie Barton's sentence. He couldn't let her hang, so he had reached a decision: break her out of her cell, then ride for the county marshal. It would place him in a poor position, arranging a jailbreak, and likely not help her case, either, but what other choice did he have? The marshal would string her up before he could ever get to the county seat and back with a stay, assuming he could even convince a higher authority she deserved a new trial.

The likelihood was strong that he would have to kill the marshal. The lawman wasn't about to let him just take her, not with his own misdeeds on the line. Lacy would have to die, too, if the little killer were with the lawdog and tried to stop him from taking Kylie.

He couldn't say the notion gave him a moment's compunction. It didn't. He reckoned the West would be better off without those two.

John went to the window, looked out into the waning afternoon. His hand rested on the butt of his Peacemaker, absently fingering the skull carving. He pondered over the best way to go about the jailbreak. He would need to arrange for his horse and one for Kylie beforehand, leave them tethered behind the marshal's for a quick getaway. He would purchase a new rifle for her as well.

He was risking his own neck and reputation, the thought occurred to him, but it mattered little. He had come to Payton's Bluff to confront his true father and find himself. Perhaps he hadn't succeeded with the latter, but the more he thought about the Barton woman the less important that goal became. Folks could find themselves in other ways; maybe that was the message his mother had truly meant for him to take from her letter.

He turned from the window, prepared to go to the livery and secure the horses so he could strike just after nightfall, but a knock on the door stopped him in the middle of the room. He tensed, knowing that this time it couldn't be Kylie. His hand slipped the Peacemaker from its holster. He eased to the door and gripped the glass handle.

He jerked the door open and swung up the Peacemaker, leveling it on the person who stood on the threshold.

A woman, a bargirl from the looks of her, let out a startled gasp. Her kohl-smudged eyes went wide.

'Who are you?' His tone came demanding, with an edge of irritation.

She stared at the Peacemaker leveled between her eyes, saying nothing until he lowered it. He slipped the weapon back into its holster. Her face relaxed a notch. A pretty blonde, she had hard features and dull eyes that hinted at some sort of addiction.

'I asked you who you were?' He folded his arms.

'I . . . I work at the saloon. Name's Trinie.'

'You best have a good reason for comin' here.'

'Christ, gent, usually menfolk ain't so unhappy to see me.' A note of pique laced her voice, chasing away any nervousness.

He frowned. 'You got business with me, state it. I ain't in the frame of mind for games, ma'am.'

She gave him a put-out look.

'Oh, hell, all right. A man named Sutter sent me to you.' She paused, as if waiting to see what effect the name had on him. It gave him a momentary start but he didn't let it show. It was the second time he'd heard the name in the last few hours. Kylie had told him Sutter was the man she went to to hire Lacy.

'Why didn't he come here himself?'

The girl looked at the floor, twisting her lips, then back up. 'He . . . he was a-feared of someone. A man named Lacy.'

Was she lying? He couldn't tell. He might have concluded she was, considering the detectable hesitation in her voice, but she appeared a bit high, so that might account for it. And what she said made sense where a man like Lacy was concerned.

'I ain't got a lot of time. Give me his message.'

'He said he has evidence that would clear that gal in the jail. He says he knows she didn't kill Ty Galendez, someone else did. Said he'd only talk to you, but he don't dare step out of his house because Lacy would kill him. Said to tell you it meant saving her life.'

He searched her face, the notion that she was lying stronger now. Suspicion clawed its way into his mind. Why would a man like Sutter get a sudden attack of conscience? What would he care about a woman who had hired him to fetch a killer? Still, if it meant even the slightest chance at

140

helping Kylie he had to take the risk that this bargirl was telling the truth. If it were a trap he reckoned he could take care of himself.

'Where?' he asked.

The bargirl smiled.

He located the place without trouble. A ramshackle shanty, it squatted on a back street near the edge of town. Taller shiplap buildings crowded around it and he saw plenty of places for a bushwhacker to hide. Just because he was willing to take a risk to clear Kylie's name didn't mean he was about to throw all caution to the wind. Damn peculiar, Stutter calling on him now, and he couldn't rule out the possibility that the marshal or Lacy had decided John Deletéreo posed too much of a danger to let him ride out, or were worried about him interfering with the execution. Sutter himself sold his morals for cash; he wasn't a man to be trusted or one likely looking for redemption.

Nerves tingling, he pressed close to a wall and observed the place for long moments. His heart stepped up a beat and muscles tensed. He was little in the mood for surveillance, but every instinct he had developed over his years of manhunting told him the girl's story stank worse than the town's piss-perfumed air.

Minutes passed. He spotted no signs of movement, no hint of anyone watching the place. That didn't mean no one was there, yet while he saw too many places a man could conceal himself, he couldn't wait forever. If the girl was telling the truth Stutter might change his mind if he got too much time to think on his decision to go against Lacy.

Deciding he'd waited long enough, he eased up to the

door. One hand on his gun butt, the other on the handle, he twisted the knob. Unlocked. The tingling in his nerves got stronger.

He gave the door an easy push, sending it creaking inward. Gloom saturated the interior and a horrendous odor of urine and garbage mixed with another foul stench assailed his senses.

'Jesus,' he muttered. Death. The odor of death. He'd smelled decomposing corpses before; the stench was one a man never forgot.

He eased inside, softly closing the door behind him. The shanty was a one-room affair, littered with waste and a few pieces of dilapidated furniture – a hardbacked chair and a rickety table, a sheetless mattress with feathers leaking from torn sides.

On the mattress lay a body.

John stared at it a moment, noting the corpse was dressed in a union suit. Bullet holes showed in the chest. He reckoned the body belonged to Sutter. Had Lacy beaten him here? Was the little killer still nearby?

John surveyed the room, making certain there were no nooks or crannies large enough to hold a man. The place was empty. If Lacy had been here he was gone now.

Stepping closer to the bed, he found the odor worse, sickening. A twinge of nausea twisted in his belly. He fought the urge to gag.

A sudden chill rode his spine as a rat scurried away from where it had been gnawing on a portion of the dead man's hand.

He knelt near the edge of the mattress, getting a closer look. Dread crept through his being. Judging by its condition, the body wasn't fresh. It had been here more than a day. The rodents had already done a sufficient job on it; bone showed through gnawed meat in places.

The only thing that kept his stomach contents from coming up was the chilling realization that if the body had been here that long the dove had been lying. Sutter couldn't have given her the message asking him to come here.

Someone else had. Someone most likely by the name of Lacy.

He sprang to his feet, warning bells clanging in his mind. Dammit, it wasn't an ambush – he was being set up.

As if in answer to that revelation the door burst open. He swung to see Marshal Studdard framed in the doorway, gun in hand.

'Don't move, Mr Deletéreo. We both wouldn't want my gun to go off accidentally.'

John's face went grim. 'Weren't satisfied with just one frame-up, Marshal? How much you being paid to bend the law every which way?'

The marshal let a loose smile turn his lips. He stepped into the shanty.

'Don't know what you are talkin' about, sir. That girl was guilty of murder. Evidence said so. Now I get a tip you lit out to kill poor Mr Sutter here and lo and behold I find I'm just a bit too late.'

'You're more than a day late. This man was dead when I got here.'

The marshal advanced another few steps. John noticed the lawdog's hand was slightly loose on the gun, trembling just a hair. He searched the marshal's eyes, seeing fear.

'Why, that's not possible. I saw Mr Sutter not more than a few hours ago at the saloon. Was bright and chipper then. I'm here to place you under arrest for murder, Mr

Deletéreo. Fact, two murders. Poor Cleatus met with his doom the other night. I got a witness that says he was headed out to talk to you.'

The trap had sprung closed and John knew it. The marshal, shaky on the gun, was a hair away from pulling the trigger if he made any sudden move. He could not draw his Peacemaker in time to prevent lead from punching into his frame.

Instead he spread his hands and sighed, taking a short step forward.

'Reckon you got me, Marshal. I s'pose there'll be a trial much like the one you gave Miss Barton?'

The marshal started to answer but never got the chance. John, in stepping forward, shifted his weight on to his back foot. He pivoted even as he completed his sentence. His foot swung up, connecting with the marshal's gun hand. The weapon went off with a flash of flame and a thunderous roar that crashed against the shanty's walls and echoed back. The bullet went wide, going clean through a wall. The recoil combined with the kick sent the gun flying from the lawdog's hand to land on the floor a few feet behind him.

The marshal's face twisted with shock, then alarm.

John seized the opportunity and flung himself at the lawdog. The marshal was faster than he expected, driven by sudden terror. He got his hands around John's neck and jammed his fingers in deep.

John snapped a short uppercut that clacked the lawdog's teeth together. Studdard's hands jerked away from John's throat and he staggered back. Recovering quickly, he looped a sloppy punch.

John ducked and the punch sailed over his head. The

manhunter countered with a blow to the marshal's belly. The lawdog let out an explosive *woof* of air and doubled.

John jerked a knee up into the man's face. Blood gushed from the man's mashed nose and he spat out a tooth.

The lawdog made a frantic grab for John's duster as he staggered backwards, but missed. John snapped up his foot, planting it squarely in the man's face.

The lawdog collapsed into a heap and rolled into a fetal position, groaning, mouth bubbling crimson.

John stood panting. He glanced around the shanty, looking for something with which to bind the lawdog. With the marshal incapacitated, things had just gotten a hell of a lot easier for breaking Kylie out of her cell – unless Lacy waited at the office.

A scuffing sound brought his attention back to the downed lawman.

The marshal had been partially faking. When he'd rolled, he'd rolled over his gun and curled into a position where he could get a hand around it. He uncoiled from that position now, murderous fury in his eyes. He swung the gun up as he thrust himself into a sitting position.

A heartbeat.

John's hand swept to his Peacemaker in a blur of motion. Pure instinct, years of experience and practice, guided his aim.

Another blast thundered through the shanty. The marshal froze in mid-aim, as a hole appeared between his eyes. He toppled backward with a heavy thud and lay still. The gun dropped from his lifeless fingers.

John stared at the dead man a moment, no remorse or regret inside him. He made a decision then. After freeing

Kylie, even if Lacy wasn't there, he was going after the little killer and bringing him back to the county marshal with them. If Lacy resisted, so much the better.

He stepped from the shanty and closed the door, certain the gunshots hadn't attracted any attention in this town. It took him only a few minutes to walk back to the marshal's office. He approached with caution, though careful not to make that obvious enough to raise the suspicions of townsfolk who might take a notion to stand up for the Galendez family and their cronies.

Casually peering into the office window, he spotted no sign of Lacy.

He entered, alert, but his readiness proved unnecessary.

Kylie's head lifted as he stepped inside, then she sprang from her cot and ran to the bars.

'John . . . the marshal and Lacy, they plan to set you up. If he finds you here—'

'Marshal won't be finding anybody . . .' His tone said it all and she nodded. He grabbed a key-ring from a wall-peg, went to the cell and unlocked the door. She ran into his arms and he held her for long moments, lost in how good it felt to have her in his arms.

'Where's Lacy?' he asked, pulling back. He could have stayed in her arms a hell of a lot longer but he had business to finish first.

'He said he was going out to the Galendez place.'

'I'm going after him. I'm taking him back to the county marshal with us. I ain't givin' him a chance to vanish into the woodwork.'

Concern sparked in her amethyst eyes.

'He won't let you just take him.'

'I'm counting on it.' A grim smile turned his lips.

Panic lit on her face, mixing with resolve.

'He's too dangerous. I'm riding out there with you. I'll take one of the marshal's rifles.'

'No, after we fetch horses you ride back to your place and collect what you want to bring. I'll meet you there.'

She shook her head. 'I'm going. I won't let you face him alone. I've got nothing left if you don't come back.'

He studied her face, deciding he could never persuade her otherwise. If he went alone she'd follow, despite his orders.

'You're a hell of a woman, Kylie Barton.' He offered her a warm look, but it was tainted by a sudden fear that he might be placing her in grave danger.

'You bet I am.' She smiled, then went to the wall rack and grabbed a rifle.

CHAPTER TEN

After securing his bay and a chestnut for Kylie, they rode for the Galendez compound. The prospect of exposing the young woman to further danger made John's nerves tighten, but she'd refused to listen to any argument that ended with her going home and waiting for his return. Her determination for seeing this through and backing him up overrode any fear and he had to admire her courage. In that way she reminded him more of Clarissa. They both had that stubborn streak; he prayed it wouldn't end in tragedy, the way it had two years ago.

The trail opened and they crossed the outer parameters of the Galendez spread. He rode a few feet ahead of her, hands tight on the reins. His gaze scanned the compound. Just how many men did Galendez have in the area? He saw none but reckoned most were about their duties or headed into town to work off steam at the saloon. Dusk already fringed the landscape. The sun had dipped below the distant mountains. Gray shadows wavered cross the grounds.

Jep would likely stay at the ranch tonight, without his brother and with Lacy. If he read the older Galendez boy right, Jep wasn't convinced Kylie was responsible for his brother's murder. But would that help when it came time to apprehend Lacy?

A rider appeared at the edge of the ranch a few hundred yards distant. Spotting them, the rider heeled his mount into a gallop with a clear intent to intercept.

John slowed up, muscles tensing and dread in his belly. Kylie drew up to his side, a questioning look on her face.

'Stay behind me . . .' he said, voice low. As the rider came closer John recognised him as Jep Galendez. The boy jerked a rifle from his saddle boot and reined up, one-handed.

John drew to halt, one hand loosening on the reins. With a slight twist of his body, his duster fell back to clear the butt of the Peacemaker.

Jep Galendez leveled his rifle on John but his gaze centered on the girl. Dark pouches had swollen beneath bloodshot eyes. He wore no hat and his dark hair rippled under the breeze.

'My brother and I might not have seen eye to eye, but he didn't deserve what he got.' Spite laced the boy's tone, which was aimed at the young woman.

She eyed the young man with resolve. Her carriage straightened.

'I didn't kill your brother, Jep. I swear I didn't.' Her voice came low, honest. 'I won't lie and tell you I didn't want him dead for what he did to me but I fully intended to send Lacy packing the night he arrived. I lost my nerve. I realized I'd made a mistake and wouldn't have gone through with it. Lacy refused to take payment and leave. He beat me and stole my money instead.'

'Why should I believe you?' Jep levered a shell into the

Winchester's chamber and shifted his aim to Kylie. John readied himself to go for his gun. He held off, knowing he had little chance of drawing before the man fired on the young woman. He hoped he could defuse the situation before it came to that.

'I don't expect you to believe me,' she said, face grim. 'None of you did before. That doesn't change the truth, though. I did not kill your brother.'

Jep stared at her, something in his gaze debating, hesitant. Doubts had surfaced, even before her words, and John reckoned the young man was basically well-intentioned, merely saddled with grief.

'What you said Ty did to you . . .' He let the words trail off.

She lowered her head, staring at the ground for a tense moment. When she looked up tears shimmered in her eyes.

'I told the truth. I don't expect you to take my word for it now any more than any of you did a month ago. But ask yourself why I'd risk calling on a killer based on a lie.'

Jep's lips tightened into a deep frown. After what seemed like an eternity, his eyes shifted to John, who held the young man's gaze with steady confidence. He saw indecision and doubt, knew the young man was struggling with his conscience. The rifle remained leveled on Kylie's chest.

'How'd she get out of jail?' He ducked his chin at Kylie.

'I got her out. The marshal decided to frame me for another killing. He and Lacy cooked it up. Lacy's a vicious killer, Jep. He ain't your friend. He's nobody's friend. He's lookin' out for himself. But I think you already know that.'

'That why you're here?' The young man's jaw muscles

rippled. His hands shook on the rifle.

'I came for him. I aim to escort him to the county marshal and see him hang for his crimes. He hurt Miss Barton twice and stole her money; only a matter of time till you or your father come in his sights next.' He paused and Jep seemed to wait expectantly for John to crystallize something of which he himself had been convinced.

'Say what you got to say, Mr Deletéreo.' Jep's voice shook and he swallowed hard.

'Don't have to, Jep. We both know Miss Barton didn't kill your brother . . . and we both know who did.'

A tear slid down Jep's face. 'I found him . . . in the tool shed. I heard a shot, but I was too far away to get there quick enough to save him. But I caught a glimpse of someone running from the place. Was too far off to tell who, but it wasn't no woman. Lacy came running up from somewhere in the direction of the house a few minutes after I got there. Said he heard the shot too and it sounded like it came from the shed. Next day, Lacy came up with Miss Barton's rifle. Said he found it hidden nearby. I was too upset to figure what a damned stupid thing it would be for her to leave it lying there after she killed my brother, 'stead of just takin' it back with her. Figure I saw runnin' from the shed didn't have no rifle, neither. Started thinkin' about it more at the trial.'

John nodded. 'Lacy's a cold-blooded killer. Don't know what business he has with your father but you can bet it ain't good.'

Jep frowned. 'He was s'posed to protect Ty but he's up to something else. That much even Ty was sure about.'

John made his voice firm. 'Let me take him, Jep. You know Kylie ain't guilty and I reckon you ain't the type to want an innocent woman's blood on your hands.'

Jep's gaze shifted to her, for a moment his expression unreadable.

'I'm sorry . . .' he whispered. 'Ty . . . he was a bastard sometimes, but he was my brother. I had to take for him, give him the benefit of the doubt, though I knew he had a bad streak.'

Kylie's eyes narrowed. 'What're you sayin', Mr Galendez?'

He gave a slight shake of his head.

'I'm sayin' I believe you and I'm sorry for what Ty did to you. I can't change it, but if there's some way I can make it up to you I will, no matter what my pa says. It's time to set things right, least as right as is possible now.'

She nodded, remaining silent.

Jep lowered the rifle and John relaxed a measure. His assessment of the boy had been right. More than that, he now had a half-brother in blood if not in name.

'I'll take you to the house . . .' Jep shoved the rifle into the saddle boot.

John shook his head. 'Lacy's basically a coward, if I read him right, but he's likely to react as a cornered animal when I come after him. Keep Miss Barton here with you until I come back. I don't return, take her to the county marshal and tell him everything before Lacy can catch up to you.'

Jep nodded. 'I'll do that, Mr Deletéreo.'

'I want to go with you.' A worried look jumped onto Kylie's features.

Pain glittered from his eyes and the memory of that day two years ago when he watched Clarissa die under a gunman's bullets flashed through his mind.

'I need you to stay here, Kylie. I'm used to handling this type situation alone. It's best that way.'

She shook her head, the tears she'd held back starting to flow.

'You got the look of someone who don't care whether he lives or dies. It's in your eyes, John. Don't try to deny it. You might think you got nothin' to lose, nothin' to come back to, but there's something if you want it . . .'

She was right. In the back of his mind, as long as she was safe he might walk into hell shooting with little regard for what happened to himself. But as his eyes locked with hers he felt something surge within him he hadn't experienced for two years, something that promised not to replace the feelings he once had, but to build upon them – if he'd let it.

'Stay here . . .' He centered his gaze straight ahead at the house a few hundred yards distant, the haunted feeling of past and present turning into one another, sweeping through his soul. He gigged his horse forward, knowing she would leave the decision to him whether Johnny Dead became a fading legend or lived again.

Fifty feet from the house a chilled determination gripped his being. He slowed his bay and hopped from the saddle, sending the horse trotting off to the right with a slap of his hand to its flank. It was a good animal. No need to risk it.

He strode towards the house, dusk taking hold. His duster swept back with the breeze and his brown eyes focused on the large windows that belonged to the drawing-room. Had he caught a glimpse of movement there?

'That's goddamn far enough, manhunter,' came a voice from within the house. He noticed then that the window had slipped open a crack.

'Lacy, I'm takin' you in.' His hand relaxed, hovering over his Pacemaker. 'No need for this to get bloody. Choice is yours.'

A harsh laugh sounded from the house.

'Just how goddamned stupid do you think I am? You got a hell of a lot of balls walkin' up to the house this way, I'll give you that. But I ain't your huckleberry, manhunter.'

John froze. A chill swept through him and something dark twisted in his belly. Images suddenly burned in his mind. He watched Clarissa die as he had a hundred times over in nightmares, the horrible scene resurrected by Lacy's single sentence.

'What?' John whispered. Then louder, 'What did you say?'

Lacy's laugh came harsher this time.

'You damn well heard me, Deletéreo. I should have done a better job two years ago, shouldn't I? But goddamn, I swore you were bleedin' your last. Hell, I even came back and visited your grave after I collected my money and killed the fella who hired me for tryin' to renege on the deal.'

'You . . .' John's mouth moved but words choked in his throat. A fever burned in his veins and rage swelled in his soul. The feeling of recognition he'd felt with Lacy all along, now it made sense. It hadn't been a substantial thing, more a whisper somewhere deep in his mind: Lacy's size, his eyes, though he had been unable truly to focus on them two years ago . . . John had retained some buried impression and that was what haunted him when he met Lacy. Close enough to touch, but too far to hold.

Here was the man who had shot him two years ago in

an ambush on the cabin. Here was the man who had killed Clarissa.

'You son of a bitch!' John yelled, fury screaming through him. 'Come out here, you bastard! Face me like a man this time!'

A gunshot answered.

Lacy grinned, seeing the manhunter frozen there like a goddamn animal in a rifle sight. He was a dead man, this time for certain. Lacy felt no compunction over shooting him right where he stood. If Deletéreo thought Lacy had any shred of honor he was permanently mistaken.

How the hell he'd managed to survive two years ago was something that Lacy could never have answered and he reckoned it didn't matter long as he finished the job now.

He leveled his Smith & Wesson on the figure standing in the yard. His finger twitched against the trigger as he took careful aim . . .

Something hit him in the back, jolting his gun arm. He jerked the trigger and the blast thundered throughout the drawing-room. The bullet went wide of the figure standing in the yard.

Lacy swung around just as a fist came towards his face. The fist struck, sending him reeling.

Payton Galendez stood there, hate in his eyes.

'I told you I wouldn't allow you to kill anybody, Lacy.' The elder Galendez had a fist cocked for another blow.

Lacy braced himself against the wall with one hand, the back of the other holding the gun wiping blood from his lips.

'Didn't seem to be a problem when that woman was gonna hang.'

'I wasn't sure she hadn't killed Ty, but I reckon now I know different, don't I?' Galendez's eyes flashed with fire.

'You stupid old man. That *hombre* out there aims to kill us both. I had him.'

'You're a yellow-bellied coward, Lacy. Go out there and face my son like a man.'

Lacy let out a scoffing laugh.

'Blood runs thick after all, don't it? You should have told him you was a proud pa when you had the chance.'

'Get out of my house, Lacy. You got no hold over me no more. Tell whoever you want what Ty was doing. The town'll treat you the same way they did the Barton woman.'

Lacy pushed himself off the wall. 'You just don't get it, do you? I ain't one of your pawns you can buy off. Gravy train ends for both of us right here.' Lacy jerked up his gun and blasted a shot. Payton Galendez's face froze with shock. He looked down at his chest where a growing scarlet stain surrounded a dark hole. His hands went to the wound as if to stanch the flow of blood pumping out but he staggered a step forward, then collapsed to his knees.

Lacy triggered another shot. Lead punched a hole through Payton's forehead.

Lacy whirled before Galendez hit the floor, going back the drawing-room window, hoping the manhunter had remained where he stood like the gallant fool he'd come as.

The yard was empty. He saw two riders approaching from the distance, a man and a woman, likely attracted by the shots.

A scuffing sound came from behind him and Lacy

spun. A man stood in the entryway, a Peacemaker in his hand.

'Oh, goddamn,' Lacy said, and started to shake.

John Deletéreo stood still, Peacemaker leveled on the boyish killer. With the first shot he'd crossed the yard to the front door and entered. He wasn't sure why Lacy had missed but didn't intend to give him a second chance.

His gaze took in the scene, instantly determining he was too late to help Payton Galendez but feeling little sympathy for the dead cattleman. Galendez had brought it on himself. His lies had caught up with him. John felt no sense of loss of a father; he'd never really had one.

Lacy stood frozen to the spot, eyes betraying fear.

'You can't just shoot me in cold blood, manhunter. You ain't got it in you. You're a man of honor.'

A thin smile turned John's lips. 'What would you know about honor, Lacy? I came here willin' to take you back to the county marshal alive. That was before I knew you killed Clarissa.'

'I saw your grave, manhunter. I saw you dyin'.' Lacy shook his head, his voice starting to shake. He was damn cold and composed when he held the advantage but with his gun loosely in his grip at his side it was another story. John took a step into the room.

'Maybe I am dead, Lacy. Maybe I've come back to haunt you. Ease that gun into your holster, slow-like.'

Lacy's eyes filled with panic.

'I won't draw on you, manhunter. You can't make me.' A dark stain appeared at the junction of his trousers.

'I'm givin' you a choice, Lacy. You can draw and have a

sportin' chance, or die where you stand. Don't matter to me.'

'That ain't no choice. You're faster than Hickok.'

'It's more choice than you gave Clarissa.' John's eyes locked with the killer's, narrowed. 'You got five seconds to holster that gun.

Lacy licked his lips, hand, trembling, lifting towards his holster, as if of its own volition.

In a frozen second, Lacy's frightened mind made the decision John had been hoping for. The little killer's gun jerked upward. A cheater to the end, he intended to catch the manhunter off guard.

John's finger feathered the Peacemaker's trigger.

The blast echoed through the room. Lacy jolted as lead punched into his chest. He never fired his own weapon. It dropped from his nerveless fingers and clattered on the floor. Lacy stumbled backward, crashing to the floor, staring straight up at the ceiling.

Silence. Deafening. John walked over to Lacy's form and knelt. The little killer gurgled something, blood bubbling from his lips.

'Not . . . your . . . huckleberry . . .' Lacy's eyelids fluttered closed. His head lolled to the side.

Too many things in John Deletéreo's life over the past two years came without satisfaction. This wasn't one of them. He'd given up hope of ever finding the man who killed Clarissa and while grief remained, knowing he'd avenged her death was a damned good feeling.

A sound came from behind him and he straightened, turning to see Jep and Kylie entering the room, both clutching rifles. Jep stared down at his father, his legs buckling and mouth opening in silent protest. Kylie ran to

John, tossing her rifle to the sofa, then clutching his waist, her head pressing to his chest.

Long minutes passed as Jep knelt beside the body of his father, saying a silent prayer. When he stood, tears shimmered in his eyes. He looked at John.

'This family's put you through more than I could ask you to forgive, both of you. I can't change what's been. But I'm tellin' you as a brother . . . as kin, John, part of this is yours now, if you want it. And, ma'am, I'll make sure the town knows what my brother did to you and try to make things better, if you'll let me.'

Kylie didn't say a word. John gave a non-committal nod and walked her from the house.

With dawn the next morning, John Deletéreo stood watching the sunrise from the edge of Kylie Barton's property. For the first time that he could recollect in two years he hadn't suffered through the nightmare of Clarissa's death. Lacy's end had brought him a measure of peace. As the sun melted the frost to drops of liquid amber, he whispered goodbye to her and knew she'd understand that he'd finally made the decision to go on living. It was what she would have wanted him to do.

Kylie Barton came up behind him, arms folded against the early morning chill. He turned to look into her eyes and offered a thin smile.

'Jep offered me a place at the Galendez home,' she said. 'Said he'd make sure I got my school teaching job back, if I wanted it.'

'Won't bring you bad memories stayin' at that place?'

She shrugged and a fragile smile came to her lips.

'Reckon it might, but Ty's gone now. He paid for what

he did. But no point stayin' there alone.' Her eyes searched his.

'Reckon having a woman around would do that place a world of good. Folks are like to talk, though.' He gave her a questioning expression.

'Let them. I stopped carin' what they thought a month ago. I guess in the end I'm not one to run from my problems. I have to face them.'

'Won't be easy. There'll be times . . .'

She frowned. 'I know . . .'

He went to her, gathered her in his arms.

'If it ever gets too much for you, just say the word and we'll ride out some place, far away from here.'

She smiled a warm smile and held tight to him.

'Time to let the past go,' she whispered.

'Reckon it is . . .' His eyelids fluttering closed, he said goodbye to the man known as Johnny Dead and let John Deletéreo begin to live again.